LOVE ACROSS THE POND

TINA GALLAGHER

TINA GALLAGHER

Broken Down in Ballyclare

Broken Down in Ballyclare

Chapter One

I TURNED off the car and sat in the driveway, too numb and exhausted to get out. The last month has been life-changing, and not in a good way. Right now, I don't want to move or function or think.

My sarcastic chuckle echoed through the car as I leaned my head back against the seat.

It's not like I have to be anywhere or do anything. Not anymore. And with Gran gone, I definitely don't want to think. Because if I do, I'll sink into a mental abyss so dark and dense, I may never resurface.

A rivulet of sweat made its way from my neck and traveled down between my shoulder blades. It's a sunny June day in Maryland outside the car, but within its confines with the windows up and the engine off, it's getting a bit stifling. I finally mustered up enough energy to open the door and welcomed the waft of cool, fresh air that flowed inside.

Grabbing my purse from the passenger seat, I stepped out of the car and slammed the door shut. I pressed my thumb against the fob and the alarm beeped behind me, mingling with the sound of my heels clicking along the sidewalk. I climbed the five steps that led me onto the porch and walked toward the front door.

I looked down at my keys and found the correct one, then pushed it into the lock and turned. As I opened the door, I smiled at the plaque that's been hanging on it forever. Most people put up shamrocks or other Irish decor around St. Patrick's Day, but the green Celtic knot plaque with *Céad Míle Fáilte* in gold lettering has hung on this door every day of the year for as long as I can remember, and even longer than that.

Blinking back tears, I opened the door and stepped inside the house. My footsteps echoed on the hardwood floors as I walked through the living room, past the dining room, and into the kitchen. I set my purse on the counter then grabbed a bottle of water from the refrigerator, twisted off the cap, and chugged half its contents in one long gulp.

Since Gran died five days ago, I've been on auto-pilot, going non-stop planning the funeral and contacting friends to let them know she was gone. Now that it's over, I feel drained in a way I never have before. I just want to crawl into bed and sleep for a week. I'm sure the shot of whiskey I downed at the after-funeral brunch isn't helping.

Most of Gran's friends may be in or past their seventh decade, but their ability to hold their alcohol is beyond impressive. They "raised their glasses to Clara" so many times, I don't know how they were still standing when we left the restaurant. Since I was driving home, I only raised one glass, but that's probably more than I should have considering I haven't really been eating or sleeping.

I finished my water then grabbed a fresh bottle and headed toward the stairs. Again, every step echoed through the house. It's amazing how empty it feels without Gran.

Just her presence filled the space with a life and warmth that just isn't here now.

Stepping into my room, I slipped out of my heels and kicked them toward the closet. I reached behind me and unzipped my dress then stepped out of it and tossed it onto the chair in the corner. Normally I'd hang it up, but right now, I really don't care if it gets wrinkled or ruined.

I pulled down my room-darkening shades and crawled into bed, pulling the blanket up over my shoulders as I curled onto my side. My body slowly melted into the mattress but my mind continued to race. I rolled to my other side, fluffing the pillow under my head, trying to get more comfortable. But even once I was as physically settled as I could be, my brain just wouldn't turn off.

Shifting onto my back, I stared at the ceiling and placed one hand on my chest and the other on my stomach then focused on my breathing like I learned to do in yoga class. Dragging a deep breath in slowly through my nose, I exhaled through my mouth, then repeated the process. I settled into a methodical in-and-out rhythm and eventually was able to calm most of my racing thoughts, but one continued to sprint through my brain…what am I going to do now?

I thought I felt lost when I was laid off from my job a month ago, but that was nothing compared to this. When Mass Organic Distribution aka MODCO let me go without warning, I was able to come home to stay with Gran, lick my wounds, and work on a plan.

Then she died.

It may sound strange to say that the death of an eighty-five-year-old woman was unexpected, but it was. Gran was so healthy and full of life. The kind of person you thought would live forever. So when I woke up five days ago and she wasn't in the kitchen reading the paper and drinking her tea, it was unusual, but I didn't expect to find her cold and lifeless in her bed.

I blinked and tears rolled down my cheeks. I've been holding them back, knowing that once I let go, I wouldn't be able to stop and I was right. Now they fell faster than I could wipe them away and I finally gave in. Rolling onto my side, I curled my knees up and just let them flow.

Huge, racking sobs shook my body as I thought about Gran. Since my parents died when I was four, she was my rock and now with her gone, I feel adrift in a way I never have before. After college, I focused on working hard and achieving my professional goals knowing that Gran was cheering me on from a distance. Now all that time away from her seems pointless. I should have been here instead of moving all around the country, climbing my way up a corporate ladder that was kicked out from under me by the people I'd made it my life's mission to impress.

I don't know how long I cried like that, but eventually the tears stopped flowing and my sobs subsided. Reaching out, I grabbed a tissue from the box on the nightstand and blew my nose. I couldn't totally clear it, but at least I was able to pull in some air. I rested my head back against the pillow, pulled the blanket over my shoulders again, and closed my eyes.

My mind still churned, but the thoughts were happier than before my crying jag. Fun memories and silly conversations floated through my brain as I drifted into that peaceful place between sleep and wakefulness. Gran had moved to the United States from Northern Ireland when she was a teenager, but much of her accent remained. Especially when she sang the Irish tunes she loved so much. I could hear her melodic voice in my head singing *Dear Old Donegal* and I sleepily hummed along.

We lived comfortably but never had the means to take

a big vacation. I always promised her that once I made enough money, I'd take her on an extended European tour and we'd spend extra time in Ireland. The sad thing is, I could have afforded to do that five years ago. I was just so focused on work, it never occurred to me to actually do it. And now I'll never get the chance. Not with Gran anyway.

My eyes popped open at that last thought and I was suddenly wide awake.

All my life, I analyzed all possible options then planned my every move and look where it got me. Maybe it's time to be spontaneous. Live on the edge. Go where the wind blows me.

I sat up, reached for my laptop, and flipped it open. After closing the resume I'd been updating, I opened Google and searched for a flight to Ireland.

IRELAND IS EVEN MORE beautiful than I imagined. Keeping my eyes on the road instead of taking in all the amazing scenery is a struggle, but I know I have to stay hyper-focused. Even though I'm finally getting the hang of driving on the wrong side of the road, it wouldn't take much for me to veer into the right-hand lane by mistake.

If I'd really been thinking, I wouldn't have rented a car at all. Hell, I wouldn't even be in this country. But planning my entire life hasn't gotten me anywhere. So when the idea to come to Ireland popped into my head, I decided to go with it and booked a flight that left twenty-four hours later. And here I am.

I spent yesterday wandering around Dublin then enjoyed fish and chips and a Guinness in a pub down the block from the bed and breakfast where I was staying. The woman sitting next to me on the plane ride "across the pond" recommended it and since I didn't have something already booked, it seemed like as good a place as any. The bed was comfortable, the breakfast hearty and delicious, and the owner even drove me to the car rental place this morning so I didn't have to take a cab. So I was happy with it.

After renting the smallest car available and purchasing every insurance offered, I hit the road, heading north toward Belfast. It was a slow-go at first and I thanked every Irish saint I could think of that I managed to rent a car with an automatic transmission because there's no way I'd be able to handle shifting on top of being on the wrong side.

The mechanical voice of the navigation app sounded over the hum of the tires letting me know to stay to the right at the split in the road coming up. I don't really have a plan, but I was given some suggestions of where to visit over breakfast and I've been venturing off the motorway to at least drive through those areas.

My one issue with this impromptu trip is that even my most casual wardrobe isn't suitable for walking across fields and wandering through ruins. My first stop was Malahide Castle where I went on a storytelling tour of the castle, walked the fairy trail, and checked out the butterfly house as well as the walled gardens. By the time I left there, my feet throbbed which limited what I did on the rest of my stops. I didn't want to get blistered feet on my first day exploring, and since it was drizzling on and off, that's exactly what would happen if I trudged along in wet chunky sandals. I'll have to pick up jeans and comfortable shoes when I stop for the night, which will be soon.

I just passed Belfast, which is only a couple of hours from Dublin via the M1, but because I've been driving as slow as possible and exited the motorway pretty often, it's been almost nine hours since I got behind the wheel of my little Ford this morning. Just thinking about that made me more tired and my jaw cracked as I yawned.

I'd traveled extensively for work for the better part of a

decade, so I could probably be certified a professional packer at this point, but for this trip, I had three options to fill my bag...bring some of my business casual items, pack the random clothes I'd left behind at Gran's through the years, or drive to the storage unit I rented and dig through the boxes stashed there to find my non-corporate duds. So I went with the lesser of three evils, which was option number one. Now I'd give anything for a pair of dry-rotting leggings and my old, ratty Converse Chucks.

But other than my packing faux pas, I've been enjoying my spontaneous trip. As someone who usually has a check-list for everything, it should have been out of my comfort zone, but it's really been great. I was never a go-with-the-flow kind of girl and always felt like if I didn't have a plan my world would fall apart. Unfortunately, that happened despite the fact that I did.

I should be home looking for a job and handling the details of Gran's estate. Yet here I am in Ireland with no return ticket home, no timeline, and no idea where I'll be tomorrow. It's actually very liberating.

At the split in the road, I veered toward the right, being extra cautious to stay in the left-hand lane in the process. Cars zipped by me but I kept my slow pace with the needle a few notches below the speed limit. I'm not looking to win any races, just get to wherever it is I'm going in one piece.

Although the day's been pretty dreary, other than some light showers, it was dry. But as I continued north, the skies darkened to a slate gray and the clouds thickened and looked more threatening. I decided to get off the next exit and look for a place to stay. I'm too tired to deal with navi-gating my way through heavy rains.

I'd just driven through a roundabout and turned onto a country road when big fat drops of rain hit my windshield a few at a time before the skies really opened up and I could barely see the hood of the car. I slowed to a crawl and fumbled with the controls before remembering how to turn on the windshield wipers. Flicking them on high, I breathed a sigh of relief when the road appeared before me again. Even though I haven't encountered a car on this road yet, I don't feel comfortable pulling over to search the navigation for a place to stay, but I'm sure I'll find something.

Humming one of Gran's favorite Irish tunes, I cautiously continued forward. This area is pretty rural and the houses are few and far between. I'm hoping to find a B&B with an available room before I break the wheel with my white-knuckled grip. Unfortunately all I've seen so far are trees and rolling hills.

I lifted my foot from the gas and slowed as I came to a fork in the road. Leaning forward, I squinted looking for a sign or road marking, but didn't see either. Not that I have a specific destination, but it would be nice to know which-ever direction I take will lead to civilization.

Following my instincts, I took the right road and breathed a sigh of relief when the rain slowed just enough so I could see a little better. I passed a pub and made a mental note of its location. I'll go another couple miles and if I don't find anything, I'll turn around and come back. If no one inside has a suggestion of where I can stay, at least I'll be able to relax and check the internet for one.

I didn't even make it another half mile before I regretted that decision and was looking for somewhere to turn around on the narrow road. The wind had picked up and leaves swirled with the rain, obstructing my vision even more. I sucked in a breath when a gust howled through the closed windows and shook the little car. Tightening my grip on the wheel, I focused on the road with unblinking eyes, following as it curved to the left.

I screamed as something appeared in my headlights. A bunch of sheep stood in the middle of the road and I slammed my foot on the brake and jerked the wheel to avoid hitting them. My tire caught the edge of the road and I turned the wheel the other way then hit a big puddle, hydroplaned, and crashed sideways through a wooden fence. The car spun as it skated through the muddy grass and I slid backwards down the hill, coming to a sudden stop against a tree.

Stunned, I sat there still gripping the wheel, frozen to the seat, blinking as I stared out my windshield. I released my fingers one by one and flexed them to make sure they still worked. I unhooked my seatbelt and rotated my neck to ease the tension there. Turning around, I looked through the cracked rear window and spotted the tree right behind my backseat.

"Well shit."

Chapter Three

I HAVEN'T EVEN HAD this car twelve hours and already managed to wreck it. And it wasn't driving on the wrong side of the road that took me down, but a gang of damn sheep. Even so, I feel lucky because it could have been a lot worse. If I crashed the car into a stone wall instead of through a wooden fence or hit the tree head-on, I'd be in a lot worse shape. I'm sure I'll be sore in the morning, but at least I don't have crushed legs or a broken nose from a deployed airbag.

My headlights cut through the rain and I spied evidence of my undignified descent all the way down the hill. From the road, it hadn't looked very steep, but from where I'm sitting now, I can see that it is. Walking back up is not going to be fun, but I'm not injured so I'll manage.

I swiped my phone open and searched for somewhere to spend the night. Unfortunately the closest place is about four miles away. Definitely walkable, but in this weather, with these shoes, I'd rather not. I decided to go to the pub and call a cab.

Reaching behind me, I grabbed my suitcase and rested

it in the passenger seat, relieved the rear window hadn't shattered. But with the rain pounding against it, there's no guarantee it will stay intact for long.

Opening my bag, I pulled out a cardigan then worked within the confines of the tiny car to put it on. A big gust of wind shook the car and I debated on whether or not I should stay put for a little while. I clicked on the weather app then cringed at the forecast. It doesn't look like this rain is going to stop for a while. I resigned myself to the fact that I'm going to have to get out and literally weather the storm.

I have an umbrella but with the way the wind is blowing, it won't be of any use. I dug around my purse and found an elastic then pulled my hair into a ponytail. At least I won't have to worry about it whipping into my eyes.

I looped my purse strap over my head so it hung across my body then grabbed the handle of my weekender bag. I'll have to forego the wheels in this mud and carry it instead. Thankfully I'm an efficient packer and only have the one piece of luggage with me.

Rain pelted against my right side as I opened the door, and I shivered at the contact. I decided to leave the headlights on and stepped out of the car then slammed the door behind me. If I turned them off, it would be nearly impossible to see through the gray skies and heavy rain. Plus, it's not like it matters if the battery dies.

I only took three steps before my left foot slid through the mud and kicked into the air, propelling the rest of me back until I fell right on my ass. My skirt flew up as I fell so the only thing between my skin and the ground was my silk underwear. Rolling onto my hip, I used the suitcase that I still firmly gripped to help me shift onto my knees and finally stand.

Shifting my weight from foot to foot, I waddled

through the mud, slowly making my way up the hill. I slipped a few times but managed to catch myself before I face-planted or slid back down. Near the top, I stepped over the wood from the broken fence then finally reached the road. Thankfully the sheep were nowhere to be seen.

Mud squished between my feet and the insoles of my sandals as I walked in the direction I'd just come from. The rain fell harder and I picked up my pace, keeping my eyes glued to the road to avoid stepping in a hole. It seemed like I was walking forever before I spotted the light from the pub's sign glowing through the streaming rain. I resisted the urge to run and instead kept my steady pace until I finally crossed the parking lot and approached the wooden door. Tugging it open, I stepped into the dim interior of the pub, relieved to be out of the rain.

Dropping my suitcase to the floor, I swiped my hands down my face then dragged them across my hair and squeezed the excess water from my ponytail. I realized the hum of voices I'd heard when I entered had quieted and I looked up to find four pairs of eyes trained on me.

Chapter Four

I PICKED up my suitcase and walked toward the bar and set it back down right behind a stool.

"Can I help ye, miss?" the bartender asked.

"I had an accident about a half-mile down the road."

His brow furrowed as his eyes skimmed down then up my body before meeting mine again.

"Are ye injured?"

"Thankfully no." Even though I did my best to squeeze my hair dry, drops of water still fell from the end of my ponytail, landing on my neck, making me shiver. "Do you have a ladies' room where I can clean up a little?"

The man at the end of the bar smiled behind his beer, but the bartender kept a straight face as he nodded toward a door across the room.

"Right over there, miss."

"Thank you."

I pulled up the handle of my suitcase and rolled it across the wooden floor toward the red door. As I stepped inside the tiny bathroom, I nearly screamed when I caught sight of myself in the mirror. I looked even worse than I'd imagined.

Mud streaked the top of my head and my ponytail hung more like limp spaghetti than hair. Remnants of mascara stained the skin under my eyes and the rest of my face was filthy despite the fact that it had been pelted by rain during the entire walk. I peeled off my ruined cashmere cardigan, revealing the sleeveless silk blouse plastered against my chest. At least the dark color isn't see-through like the mud-caked ivory ruffle wrap skirt that's dripping wet and sticking to my legs.

After turning on the water, I pumped liquid soap into my hand and washed my arms then my hands, watching the surface of the white sink turn brown as I rinsed off. Leaning forward, I held my hands together and put them under the water, then splashed it over my face, repeating the process three more times before it was passably clean.

Double-checking that the door was locked, I unwrapped my skirt and squeezed it out over the sink then hung it on the hook on the wall. Normally I'd never put my bare feet on the floor of a public restroom, but I didn't really have a choice. I leaned forward and unbuckled my sandals then stepped out of them. Using several wet paper towels, I cleaned the worst of the dirt from them and my feet.

I stepped out of my underwear and gave my legs and ass the same treatment. I'd love nothing more than to throw the scrap of silk away, but there's no way I could go commando with my wet skirt. So once I cleaned myself and my panties the best I could, I put them back on and wrapped my skirt around my waist. I still looked like something the cat dragged in, but at least my skin wasn't caked with dirt anymore.

I stepped back into my sandals and buckled them,

cringing when I spotted the mud scattered over the tile floor. Grabbing the handle of my weekender bag, I unlocked then opened the door and walked out of the bathroom. The conversation stopped when they noticed me, leaving no doubt in my mind that I'd been the topic.

Stopping just outside the door, I said, "I left mud all over the floor. If you give me a mop, I'll clean it up."

The bartender waved me toward the bar.

"Come and sit," he said. "I'll need ta be cleanin' the rest of the place anyway."

Making my way across the room, I settled onto a stool and rested my elbows on the bar.

"I took the liberty of callin' the Doherty boys fer ye."

The dirty boys?

I must have looked as confused as I felt because the bartender continued.

"They own a garage and will tow yer car and take ye wherever yer goin'. Within reason, of course." He finished drying the glass in his hand and placed it under the bar. "Actually, it's just Conor. Paddy's retired and the rest of the boys are doin' other things now. Brady runs the bar, Ronan is a handyman and works with the horses." He frowned and looked toward the men sitting at the bar. "Lord help me, I still dunno what young Mac does."

"Something with the computers," a man with thick white hair and a ruddy complexion said.

That led to a discussion about what exactly "young Mac" did with "the computers" and I listened to them, trying to figure out what they were saying half the time. And when one of the men spoke, I realized the bartender had been saying Doherty boys and not dirty boys. Which made a lot more sense.

The bartender turned his attention back to me.

"At any rate, Conor will be here when he can." He

scratched his bald head and smiled. "Since you'll be here a little bit, we might as well get friendly. This here is Jack Higgins, Shane O'Donnell, and me brother, Marty Kelly. And I'm Jamie Kelly. I own this place."

I smiled and nodded at each man in turn then glanced at the mirror behind the bar etched with a shamrock with Kelly's written in the middle then met Jamie's gaze again.

"Ruby Devlin."

"Can I get ye a drink, Ruby Devlin?"

I almost told him I wanted a Guinness but changed my mind at the last minute.

"I'll have a Bushmills. Neat."

Arching his brow, he quickly filled a small tumbler with whiskey then placed it in front of me on top of a cork coaster.

"Thank you."

I took a quick sip, then a longer one savoring the sharp floral flavor and vanilla undertones before setting the glass down again.

"So where are ye from?" Jack asked.

"Maryland originally but for the past ten years or so, I've lived all over the United States."

"So what brings ye ta Ireland?" Marty asked.

I thought about Gran and decided to answer with a half-truth.

"I've always wanted to visit and the timing was right."

"And what made ye decide ta rent a car?" Shane asked with a smile.

"I figured it was the best way to explore." I finished my whiskey and pushed my glass toward Jamie, tapping the rim, letting him know I want another. "It didn't take me too long to get the hang of driving on the other side of the road." Jamie placed the glass in front of me again and I took a long drink, enjoying the warmth spreading through my belly. "I was even handling it when the storm started and then I drove around a curve and saw a bunch of sheep and swerved to miss them."

Jamie looked at the men. "Johnny Griffith's flock must a busted out again."

My head felt pleasantly buzzed and I realized I hadn't eaten since noon. Which would've been fine if I wasn't on my second whiskey.

"Do you have some chips or something? I haven't eaten in a few hours and this whiskey is going right to my head."

He reached below the bar and tossed a bag in front of me.

"The only thing I have are crisps."

I grabbed the bag and opened it. "Sorry, that's what I meant."

Reaching inside, I pulled out two chips...I mean crisps...shoved them into my mouth and chewed.

"So where are ye stayin'?" Jamie asked.

I shrugged and swallowed.

"I'm not sure. I found a place on the internet about four miles from here and was hoping to get a room there." I picked up my phone. "In fact, I should call to see if they have space."

"If yer talkin' about The Blackburn Inn, it's closed."

"Closed?" He nodded and I looked at my screen then turned it so he could see. "It says here, it's open."

"And yet, it ain't," he said. "There was a fire a while back so it's bein' repaired."

An old-fashioned ringtone sounded and I realized it was actually the wall phone across the bar. Jamie picked up the receiver then put it back in place almost immediately.

"Conor is on his way," he said.

I ate a few more crisps, thankful I didn't decide to walk to the inn instead of coming here. Finishing my whiskey, I enjoyed the fuzzy feeling in my head. It'd been a long day. Hell, it'd been a long month and an even longer week. I'd love to have another whiskey to enhance the buzzed feeling even more, but I needed to figure out where I'm staying. Suddenly being without a plan didn't seem like such a good idea.

The door behind me opened, letting in the sounds of the storm.

"Ah, there he is," Jamie said.

I looked over my shoulder and saw the most beautiful man I'd ever seen step inside the pub. He swiped back his wet brown hair and shook the excess water off his raincoat. Tingles zinged between every erogenous zone in my body when his gray eyes met mine.

"Oh wow."

Chapter Five

I WANTED to suck those words back in but the best I could hope for was that no one heard them. The sound of low laughter from the other end of the bar let me know they had.

Conor frowned over at the men then looked at me again.

"I'm guessin' yer the one needin' the tow."

The gravelly tone of his voice kicked the impact of his accent up several notches making him that much more attractive. I nodded, not trusting myself to speak as he walked toward me.

Leaning his elbow against the bar, he said, "Ye can show me where the car is and I'll hook it then take ye wherever yer stayin'."

Before I could answer, Jamie spoke for me.

"She doesn't have a place ta stay."

"What de ye mean?"

"Just what I said."

"You don't have a place ta stay?" he asked me.

I shook my head, feeling very foolish. Apparently I'm

not the kind of woman who can live on the edge. Sure, hopping on a plane with no plan was thrilling for a minute, but now I'm stuck in a pub, on a rainy night, with nowhere to go. No wonder these guys are looking at me like I've lost my mind.

"Apparently the place I'd hoped to stay isn't open at the moment." I picked up my phone and swiped it open. "But I'm open to any suggestions."

Conor's brow furrowed and he swiped his hair back off his forehead again.

"I might know of a place close by."

He pulled his phone out of his back pocket and dialed as he stepped away from the bar then walked toward the window on the other side of the room. My head doesn't usually get turned by a pretty face, but I couldn't stop myself from twisting my neck to watch him over my shoulder. His straight nose, perfect cheekbones, and strong jaw looked just as good in profile as they did head-on.

I strained my ears to listen to what he was saying but couldn't hear exact words, just the sexy cadence of his voice. When I heard Jamie and the guys start talking about the weather, I turned my head to pay attention. Apparently the heavy rain is going to stick around all night.

Before I could check my phone to validate their words, Conor returned to my side.

"Yer set fer a place ta stay," he said.

I should probably have asked for specifics but I was too exhausted to care, not to mention buzzed. Plus, I really want to get out of these wet clothes and take a hot shower. The nooks and crannies that are caked with mud are becoming really uncomfortable.

"Great." I smiled and Conor blinked, seeming to freeze in place before taking a step back. "It was nice meeting all of you." I glanced down the bar at Shane, Jack, and Marty then back at Jamie. "Thank you so much for your help."

"Yer more than welcome," he said.

I stood and reached for my bag, but Conor grabbed it then gestured toward the door.

"After you."

Conor followed me out of the bar and I was happy to see he'd parked right outside the door. The rain was still really coming down and I'd hate to get totally drenched again walking any distance.

He reached around and opened the passenger door for me. I climbed in and clicked my seatbelt into place then glanced over as Conor opened the back driver's side door and set my bag on the seat before slamming it closed. The front door quickly opened and he settled in behind the wheel.

"I didn't see anythin' on my way here so I'm guessin' yer car is ta the right."

I nodded as he started the truck.

"About a half-mile down the road. Just after you go around the curve, you'll see the broken fence on the left."

He pulled out of the lot and slowed down as we neared the spot. Once he saw the broken fence, he angled the truck so the lights shined down the hill. It's dark down there so I'm guessing the battery on my rental died.

"I'm gonna back down and hook it." He looked over at me and smirked. "Hold on."

Thankfully he'd decided to back down because other-wise, the trip would have been much more jarring. This way, I just rested against the seat and held the handle over my door to keep from falling into the console when we went over the worst of the bumps.

Once we got to the bottom, Conor shifted the truck into park. He reached his left arm behind my seat and retrieved a hard hat with a light attached. After placing it on his head, he unhooked his seatbelt then zipped his raincoat.

"Do you need help?"

He shook his head and opened the door.

"I'll be right back."

That said, he stepped out and slammed the door behind him.

I shifted my gaze between the side and rearview mirrors, watching the light and his shadowy figure move back and forth in the small space between the truck and car. Conor stood just behind the truck and I heard the whirring sound of a motor. In the light from his helmet, I watched the front end of the car rise until it hung by the thick chain attached to his truck.

Conor got back behind the wheel. He tossed his hat into the back then unzipped the raincoat and peeled it off, leaving it behind him against the seat.

"Ye sure yer not hurt?" he asked. "It looks like ye hit that tree pretty hard."

"I'm fine. If I hit it head-on, it would have been much worse."

"Can't argue with that."

He shifted the car into drive and we slowly made our way up the hill. The tires skidded in the mud but Conor expertly maneuvered the truck so we didn't get stuck. I breathed a sigh of relief when we pulled onto the road.

"So what threw ye off, the storm or the curve in the road?"

"Neither. I swerved to keep from hitting a gang of sheep in the middle of the road."

"Flock."

"Excuse me?"

"It's not a gang of sheep, it's a flock."

That's *not* what I thought he said.

"Oh."

We drove in silence for a few miles, the rhythmic sound of the windshield wipers making me sleepy. Shaking my head, I sat up straighter in my seat. I didn't want to conk out before we reached our destination.

"Thank you for towing the car and finding me a place to stay."

"It was no trouble at all." He blended the last two words together so it sounded like he said a-tall. "It can stay at my garage until you talk ta the rental company and they say what ta do with it." Again the last two words blended together.

"I appreciate it."

I was thinking of a tactful way to ask exactly where I'll be spending the night, but before I came up with something, he flipped on his left blinker. I looked in that direction and didn't see anything but trees. He turned and the headlights flashed across a road, which he pulled onto.

We drove a few feet and I realized the road was actually a driveway when a large two-story house appeared in front of us. The lights on the first floor glowed through the windows and a spotlight kicked on as we followed the circular driveway to the front of the house.

The door opened and a woman stood just inside waving, so at least she's expecting us.

"Head inside. I'll get yer bag."

I unhooked my seatbelt and thanked him again.

Rain pelted me as soon as I opened the door then slammed it behind me after I jumped out of the truck. I ran through the puddles toward the door and the woman stepped aside and ushered me in.

"Oh, look at ye," she said. "Come in."

She put her arm around my shoulders to guide me into

the impressive foyer. I resisted and she looked over at me with a frown.

"I don't want to mess up the floor."

"Don't ye be worryin' about that. This old house has seen its fair share a messes fer sure." This time when she urged me forward, I went. "I'm Fiona Doherty."

"Ruby Devlin."

Conor came through the door and closed it behind him. He set my bag on the floor and

shrugged out of his raincoat and hung it on the rack in the corner then took off his boots.

"Yer a fine mess," Fiona said to him.

He smiled, flashing straight white teeth.

"Thanks Ma." He leaned down and kissed her cheek. "Where should I put Ruby's bag?"

Ma?

Now that I'm paying attention, it's pretty obvious that Conor has her eyes. And she did say her last name is Doherty.

"She'll be stayin' in the pink room."

"Of course she will."

"You follow Conor to yer room and get cleaned up. I'll make ye somethin' ta eat."

"You don't have to go to any trouble. I'm fine," I said, but my growling stomach sounded at her words making a liar out of me.

Fiona smiled and walked down the hall leaving me alone with her son.

"This way." He picked up my bag and used it to gesture toward the stairs.

I followed him up the large staircase, taking in the family photos lining the walls. Even more were displayed on the walls and tables in the large landing on the second floor and continued down the hallway. I spotted Conor in quite a few and made a mental note to study them better on my way downstairs.

There didn't seem to be any other guests. The rooms we passed were all empty.

"Here ye are."

Conor stopped outside the last room on the right and reached inside to turn on the light then gestured for me to enter. My eyes widened as I looked around at the ultra-feminine space.

I heard a low chuckle from just behind me and I glanced over my shoulder.

"It's somethin', right?"

Taking in the pink walls, carpet, curtains, and bedding, broken only by an occasional splash of white, I said, "It definitely is something."

"After havin' four boys, Ma hoped for a girl, but it never happened. But that didn't stop her from decoratin' this room just in case." He looked around the space before meeting my gaze again. "Now she's hopin' for a grand-daughter. Although at this point, a boy will do just as well for her. She's gettin' desperate."

Something didn't make sense.

"This is a bed and breakfast, right?"

He shrugged and tilted his head from side to side.

"Not exactly."

"What *exactly* does that mean?"

"Ma always says she's sick a roaming around this big house and that she's gonna turn it into one. So when you needed a place ta stay, I figured it's good practice for her."

"Conor!" He lifted his right brow. "I can't believe you just brought me here to stay at your mother's house."

"She's thrilled. Couldn't ye tell?"

"But…"

"But?"

"I can't just stay at your mom's house."

"Why not?" I couldn't think of a good reason so I just stayed quiet. "Bathroom's through that door," he said pointing across the room. "It's got more pink I'm afraid."

At this point, I don't care what color it is as long as it has a shower so I can clean up properly.

"Don't be overthinkin' it. Ma is thrilled you're here."

I thought about Fiona's warm greeting and figured it'd be okay to stay for the night. Tomorrow I can get a new rental car and be on my way.

Chapter Six

FIONA WAS STIRRING something on the stove when I entered the kitchen. She looked over at me and smiled.

"Don't you look lovely?" She turned a knob and the flame under the pot disappeared. "Have a seat. I heated up some potato and leek soup and made you a sandwich." She nodded at the plate on the table.

"Thank you so much, but you didn't have to go through so much trouble."

"It's no trouble. You've had quite the night." She ladled soup into a bowl then placed it

beside the sandwich. "Sit and eat. Ye must be starvin'."

I did as I was told, picked up the sandwich, and took a big bite.

"Mmm, this is delicious," I said then took another bite.

"Would ye like a wee cup a tea?"

My mouth was still full, so I just nodded. She filled a white porcelain cup from the teapot on the counter, set it in front of me, and settled into the chair adjacent to mine.

"Yer hair is such a beautiful color."

"Thank you."

I used to hate when people commented on my strawberry-blonde hair, but now I don't mind. At least I don't have to spend hundreds of dollars a month at a salon like some of the women I know. Other than washing and getting it trimmed occasionally, my hair is pretty much maintenance-free.

The pale skin that accompanies the hair still annoys me, but other than dousing myself in sunblock to avoid burning, there's not much I can do about it. At least the freckles I'd had as a child have faded...for the most part anyway.

I finished the sandwich and moved onto the soup. The first spoonful warmed my belly and I quickly took a second.

"Are ye sure yer not hurt?" Fiona asked.

I nodded. "Just embarrassed."

"Why's that?"

"Driving off the road and smashing my rental car my first day in Ireland isn't something to be proud of."

"Exactly what has a pretty girl like you wanderin' around Ireland with no place ta stay?"

I shoved the last spoonful of soup into my mouth and shrugged as I swallowed.

"I've always wanted to visit Ireland and the timing was right, so I booked a last-minute flight. Wandering around the countryside with no real plan seemed like an adventure." I took a sip of tea. "And it probably wouldn't have been a problem if I didn't run into that ga—flock of sheep and run off the road."

"Johnny Griffith's sheep are a menace, fer sure."

Fiona made me feel so welcome, I forgot that her son basically stuck her with me for the night.

"I want to thank you for taking me in. When Conor said he knew a place I could stay, I thought he meant a hotel or bed and breakfast. I didn't realize he was bringing me to your home."

"Don't ye be worryin'." She reached out and squeezed my hand. "We're glad ta have ye."

"I'll call the rental company first thing tomorrow and get a new car then I'll be out of your hair."

"We'll see about that when the time comes," she said. "Rest assured, yer welcome ta stay here as long as ye need. The good Lord knows there's plenty a room now that the boys moved out and it's just Paddy and me ramblin' about."

"The house is beautiful."

That's definitely a true statement but I could see how the place would seem empty with just two people living here.

"It's been in my husband's family for years."

"Conor said you're thinking about opening a bed and breakfast."

"I keep tellin' them I am because none of the lot have givin' me grandbabies yet. I need somethin' to fill my time."

That's the second time I've heard about her lack of grandchildren since I got here. Which makes me wonder if her sons are married. Well, one son in particular anyway.

There's just something about Conor that draws me to him. I'm not normally into one-night stands or casual flings, but I'd definitely make an exception for him.

"Do your sons all live nearby?"

She nodded.

"Conor lives above the garage just down the road. Brady lives above the bar not too far from that." Fiona pointed toward the window over the sink. "Ronan lives above the stables and Mac just bought a cottage not too far from the garage." She sighed. "Mac was engaged but I dunno what happened with that. They parted ways last year. And the other three haven't brought home a girl in years."

I know that doesn't mean Conor isn't seeing anyone, but if he's not bringing her home, it can't be too serious. Of course, that doesn't mean he'd be interested in getting with me, but at least if I decide to go for it and he's not, I can leave town and not have to face him again.

Instead of deciding if I have the guts to act on my attraction, I kept the conversation focused on Fiona.

"It's nice that they're so close," I said.

"It is, and I know I'm luckier than most. A lot of the young people move away and their parents only see them once a year or so. I see mine most every day."

My chest tightened at the thought of all the years I spent moving all over the country. Some years I didn't see Gran in person for months, just via FaceTime.

"Everything all right?" Fiona asked and I nodded. "Ye sure? Yer face went pale all of a sudden."

"I'm just tired. I think everything that happened today finally caught up with me."

"You go get some sleep. Tomorrow is a new day."

I smiled and said good night then made my way upstairs. After brushing my teeth, I slipped under the pale pink comforter and settled into bed. I have no idea if the mattress was that comfortable or if I was that tired and mentally drained, but I fell asleep within a matter of minutes.

Chapter Seven

I DON'T NORMALLY SLEEP MORE than four hours a night so between jet lag and going to bed early, I thought I would have been up in the middle of the night. But I opened my eyes to a gray, but bright sky feeling fully rested. Which was a good thing because I have a lot to do and figure out.

After showering, I put on a gray pencil skirt, floral blouse, and a thin salmon-colored cardigan. My chunky sandals were still wet, so I slipped my feet into a pair of black ballet flats. I really need to go shopping for more casual clothes and appropriate shoes.

But first things first. I picked up my phone and called the rental company. After a ridiculous number of rings, I was prompted to leave a message at the beep. I'd hoped to have a plan before going downstairs, but I guess that will have to wait.

I checked myself in the mirror one last time and headed out of my room. On my way downstairs, I studied the countless pictures lining the hallway. Both portraits and candid shots were lovingly displayed in frames, none of which matched, but somehow blended perfectly together.

Conor and his brothers look alike enough that you'd know they're related. And I imagine poor Fiona had her hands full raising them because all four have the devil in their eyes.

My mouth watered as the most amazing smells floated upstairs pulling my attention from the pictures. I hope Fiona isn't cooking a full breakfast on my account. Just letting me stay here is above and beyond.

I heard voices as I made my way down the stairs and they got increasingly louder with every step I took. As I rounded the corner into the kitchen, I stopped, eyes wide. The table I'd sat at last night with Fiona was now covered with platters of eggs, bacon, sausage, and potatoes as well as bread, butter, and marmalade.

The five men seated at the table were eating, talking, and laughing while Fiona stood, leaning against the counter, watching her brood. I must have made a noise because her eyes shifted in my direction.

"Ruby, come have a seat," she said, then pulled out the chair next to Conor.

Even over the smell of breakfast, his fresh scent tickled my nose as I sat.

Fiona introduced me to Brady, Ronan, Mac, and her husband Paddy. The Doherty men are a good-looking lot for sure and it's pretty obvious they're very close. It was just always Gran and me and I've always wondered what it would be like to have a big family like this.

"Help yerself," Fiona said, as she set a steaming cup of tea in front of me before taking the seat across from her husband at the head of the table.

The bacon, sausage, and potatoes were directly in front of me so I put each on my plate.

"Conor, pass her the eggs," Paddy said.

He did as he was told and held the platter as I took a spoonful.

"Thank you."

He smiled in response then put the platter back on the table and continued eating his breakfast.

"I hope you didn't do all this on my account," I said to Fiona.

"Whatever do ye mean?" she asked.

I gestured toward the feast in front of me with my fork. "All this food."

"Oh deary, that's just breakfast."

"You make this every day?"

She nodded and I looked around as the men all did the same.

"Of course there's more on Sunday. Usually a quiche, assorted pastries, and scones with clotted cream."

"Oh wow."

"I enjoy cookin'," she said. "Plus it keeps this lot coming 'round so it's worth it."

"We'd come visit ye anyway, Ma," Ronan said.

That led to a lively discussion about how much or little time Fiona sees her sons. I enjoyed the banter as I cleared my plate. Beyond the occasional bagel or oatmeal, I'm not usually much of a breakfast eater, but I found myself reaching for seconds. With this helping, I also took a thick slice of bread and slathered it with butter and orange marmalade. Maybe it's the fresh air that's making me so hungry.

"Ye live on the other side of the yard and I see you the least, Ronan Doherty."

"I'm busy with workin' and takin' care of the horses, but still manage to get here at least once a day."

"Hmmph."

I'd just swallowed a bite of sausage when my phone rang.

"I'm so sorry, I need to take this. It's the rental car company. I left a message for them before I came down."

"Ye can take it in the office," Fiona said. "It's the door on the left just before the entrance hall."

I stood and thanked her then swiped my phone to answer as I walked out of the kitchen.

"Hello."

"Ruby Devlin?"

"Yes, hi."

I peeked into the room on my left and entered when I spotted the big desk in the center.

"My name is Lara Black. I received your message about the accident you had with your rental car. I'm happy to hear you weren't injured in the crash."

"Thank you. I was very lucky."

"I'll just need to confirm some information and get some more details."

Lara spoke with a very proper British accent and as she asked me questions about me and

the accident, I felt like I was being interrogated by the headmaster of a swanky boarding school.

My footsteps were muffled on the plush burgundy carpet as I paced in front of the couch at the back of the room, filling her in on what had happened.

"Thankfully you had the foresight to purchase our best coverage so you won't be financially responsible for anything."

I let out a relieved breath at her words. I'd grilled the man at the rental counter to make sure I wouldn't have to pay out of pocket if I had any issues with the car, but you never know. It's not uncommon to be promised one thing when purchasing insurance to be told something else when you need to cash in on the policy.

"That's good to hear," I said. "I'm currently in Ballyclare. Would I need to go back to Dublin to get a replacement car or can I pick one up closer to here?"

"Unfortunately, there's an issue with a replacement."

"What kind of issue?"

"We don't have a vehicle available at the moment."

"What do you mean?"

"Just what I said. Our entire fleet is either rented out or being maintained."

"How is that even possible?"

"In all honesty, I've worked for this company for twelve years and have never seen this happen."

Lucky me.

"So what do I do now?"

"I'm working to get you a car elsewhere but with the insurance, it's an involved process and will take a few days. I can't promise I'll have it resolved by the weekend."

"Can I just rent a car here?"

"If you'd like but it won't be covered," she said then offered more details of the process. "Do you have any questions?" she asked when she finished.

"No."

The single-word answer was all I could muster.

"Then I'll call you when I have more information."

I'm not a "kill the messenger" kind of person, so I thanked her and said I'd be waiting to hear back from her. Disconnecting the call, I sank onto the couch and rubbed my temples.

I'd wanted an adventure and this is for sure turning into an epic one.

Chapter Eight

"HOW'D YE DO?" Fiona asked as I entered the kitchen.

I settled into the chair between her and Conor again and shook my head.

"They don't have a replacement car right now so I'll have to wait a couple of days, possibly through the weekend."

"What do ye mean they don't have a car?" Conor asked.

"She said their entire fleet is let out or being maintained."

I detailed some more of the conversation, still unable to believe it. Seriously, what are the chances? After splurging on insurance to avoid any other costs, I'd hate to shell out more money for another car, but I don't have much choice. Hopefully it will only be for a couple of days until Lara gets everything straightened out on her end.

"Do you know anywhere I can rent a car?" I asked Conor.

Before he could answer, Fiona spoke.

"There's no need ta do that. Stay here 'til the company has one available."

"Oh no, I couldn't do that."

"Why ever not?" she asked.

"This is your home. You've already been so generous, I couldn't ask to stay any longer than I have."

"Ye didn't ask, Fiona offered," Paddy said then looked at his wife and winked. "Trust me when I tell ye that she's thrilled someone is usin' that room yer in."

Aside from the fact that it would just be easier to stay, it's nice here. I feel comfortable and definitely welcome. Plus I'd get to see Conor some more, which is a big plus. I just need to quiet the cynical American in me and accept Fiona's hospitality.

Conor nudged my arm with his elbow drawing my attention his way.

"It's fine. Really."

I looked into his gray eyes and got lost in the attraction that flowed hot and strong between us. I'm not sure how long we sat there just staring at each other, but it was long enough for his brothers to notice and start snickering across the table.

"Enough with ye," Fiona said to them.

With the spell between Conor and me broken, I shifted in my seat and looked at her.

"I appreciate your offer and I accept. But you have to let me help you around the house and if at any time having me here is a nuisance, you'll tell me and I'll leave."

She patted my hand then squeezed.

"It'll be a joy ta have ye here."

I noticed that she didn't exactly agree to my terms, but I'll just make sure to pitch in and won't stay long enough to overstay my welcome.

"Once we clean up after breakfast, I'd like to go shopping for some casual clothes and comfortable shoes," I said. "Is there a store in walking distance? Or I could call a cab if I have a destination in mind."

"No need for either," Fiona said. "Conor can take ye wherever ye need ta go."

Based on the twinkle in her eyes and the eager way she'd spoken the words, my guess is she's playing match-maker. Which I wouldn't have a problem with if she'd be happy with Conor and me spending time together for the rest of my stay. But I'm sure she's imagining something more long-term.

"Don't you have to work?" I asked Conor, hoping he'd offer a reason for not accompanying me.

He shook his head. "Nothin' today and if there's an emergency, they'll call Brody at the bar if no one answers at the garage."

So much for that.

Which is how, an hour later, I ended up in the passenger seat of Conor Doherty's car. The interior is much smaller than the tow truck's and our shoulders brushed more often than not when he rounded a bend or drove over a bump in the road. At first I held myself stiff trying to avoid touching him, but then decided to just relax and go with it.

"So if ye don't mind me askin', why'd ye pack so fancy?"

"A lot of my clothes are in storage and since I booked the trip last minute, I didn't have time to go get them. I brought the most casual things I had on hand and hoped they'd work. It didn't take me long to figure out that they wouldn't. If nothing else, I need sturdier shoes if I'm going to explore."

"Why was the trip last minute?"

I debated on how to answer then just decided to go with the truth.

"A couple reasons. I was let go from my job a month ago so I had the time, but mostly because my Gran died last week."

Conor shifted his eyes in my direction for a second before putting them back on the road.

"I'm sorry fer yer loss."

"Thank you."

My voice sounded hoarse and I swallowed to clear the lump that had formed.

"Were ye very close?"

I nodded even though his attention was on the road.

"She raised me. My parents died in a car accident when I was four so it was just the two of us."

"Jesus, Mary, and Joseph. I'm sorry."

Those were the last words spoken until we reached our destination.

———

THE STRIP MALL Conor took me to had everything I needed. A lot of the stuff was on sale too so it was a win-win. I'll have to buy another suitcase to get my new clothes home, but I'll worry about that when the time comes.

I'd expected him to wait in the car while I shopped, but he'd followed me from store to store and even carried my bags. Once I'd gotten everything I needed and more, he suggested we get some ice cream.

I wasn't really hungry after my big breakfast, but he's been such a good sport, I couldn't say no. So I followed him into an adorable, old-fashioned ice cream shop. He ordered a hot fudge sundae and I kept it simple with a single scoop of salted caramel ice cream.

"So why Ireland?"

It took me a second to realize he was picking up our conversation from earlier.

"My Gran is—was from Ireland. She grew up in Derry."

"Do ye still have family there?"

"Gran was an orphan so as far as I know, no. My grandfather is from Derry as well, but I don't know much about him. He died when my dad was young and Gran never really talked about him."

He nodded, acknowledging my words, then continued to eat his sundae.

"How long're ye here for?"

"I'm not sure. I bought a one-way ticket."

"You really did come without a plan."

"It seemed like a good idea at the time but now, not so much." I let out a sarcastic laugh. "I've *never* done anything that didn't involve a plan and at least one backup plan. After losing my job and then Gran, I obviously had some sort of nervous breakdown."

"Or maybe ye just started trustin' yer instincts and ended up where yer meant ta be right now."

"Is that what you do? Just trust your instincts?"

"Fer the most part."

"And things just work out?"

"Ya they do," he said then placed the last spoonful of sundae into his mouth. After he swallowed, he added, "And if they don't, they weren't meant ta be."

"So you're saying that if something doesn't happen, it just wasn't meant to be?"

"Ye can't just sit on yer arse and expect things ta come yer way, but ya. Yer wastin' yer energy tryin' ta control the universe."

"Well, until last week, I planned everything I wanted and worked to make it all happen."

"That may be true, but when ye lost yer job and yer gran died, ye didn't plan. Ye just acted on instinct and here ye are."

"Then I crashed the car and was stuck with nowhere to stay in the middle of a downpour."

"All that could a happened if ye'd had a grand plan."

I thought about that then shrugged.

Conor stood, obviously pleased that he'd made his point and I followed him out of the

ice cream shop. He opened the passenger door for me then rested his elbow against the roof and leaned forward after I settled into my seat.

"Whether ye planned to be here or not, I'm glad ye are. It would a been a shame if we'd never met, Ruby Devlin."

After flashing a sexy smirk, he slammed the door shut. I watched him walk around the front of the car, admiring his lean muscular frame.

It would have been a shame indeed.

Chapter Nine

I DON'T KNOW how Fiona Doherty could ever complain that her house is too quiet. She's had more people visit in the forty-eight hours I've been here than Gran and I had in a year. Friends and family just randomly pop in for "a wee cuppa" and to chat. When I left the house earlier, she and her two sisters were sitting around the table discussing what to do for their father's upcoming seventy-fifth birthday.

After chatting for a few minutes, I left them to it and went for a walk. The sun had finally made an appearance, so I spent most of the morning exploring the extensive grounds. That led to meeting the horses and watching Ronan conduct two lessons. One of which was with a woman who was obviously more interested in him than learning how to ride and kept shooting me dirty looks.

Now, it's just past noon and as I walked by the three-season room, Fiona knocked on the window and waved me inside. She and three other women sat in the oversized chairs, their knitting needles making a light clicking sound.

Without missing a beat, Fiona introduced me to her friends Mary, Chelsea, and Noelle.

I sat next to her and watched, fascinated, as each woman's hands moved in an easy rhythm turning the single strands of yarn that emerged from the bags at their feet into something beautiful.

"Do ye knit?" Noelle asked.

"No. My Gran used to enjoy tatting and crocheting but I never sat still long enough to learn how to do anything beyond how to make a single strand," I said. "Now I wish I'd learned."

"Well, it's never too late ta start," Fiona said. "I was never good at tatting and I don't have a crochet hook handy, but I can teach ye how ta knit."

She reached into her bag and pulled out a ball of slate gray yarn and two needles. After handing them to me, she pulled two more needles and another ball of yarn from her bottomless bag and demonstrated how to hold the needles properly and cast on. It took multiple tries and a lot of coaching from Fiona and the other women, but I was finally able to mimic what she did and soon I had my first row and was onto the second.

"So where'd ye wander this morning?" she asked.

"Just around the grounds and I sat by the pond for a while then met Ronan's horses and watched him give a couple lessons."

"It's such a lovely day, it's a shame yer stuck here."

I looked up and saw the four women exchange smiles. Fiona obviously has something in mind, but I'm not going to ask. I'm sure I'll find out what she's thinking eventually. Shifting my gaze back to my hands, I focused on making my stitches as even as possible.

Fiona stood and set her knitting on the chair.

"I'll be right back, ladies. Does anyone be needin' anythin' while I'm up?"

We all said we didn't and she left us to our knitting. I

have to say, I'm happy with the progress I'm making on my scarf. I have several rows in place. They're not perfect, but I think they're pretty good for my first attempt.

"Yer catchin' on," Chelsea said, echoing my thoughts.

"This is fun. What are you all making?"

"A throw blanket for my son and his new wife," Mary said. "It's the Cassidy clan pattern."

After admiring her work, I looked at Noelle.

"If I ever get these shoulders right, this'll be a sweater."

Other than the fact that the item she held up didn't have sleeves, it looked like something I could buy from the Irish goods store back home.

"Mine is just a cabled shawl," Chelsea said.

Just.

Fiona returned and settled back into her chair looking quite pleased with herself. Her smug smirk was explained a little while later when a fresh-from-the-shower Conor arrived. I wanted to be annoyed, but he looked too adorable with his damp hair and ruddy cheeks. After greeting the ladies, he turned to me.

"Ruby, I'm done workin' fer the day and was wonderin' if you'd want ta go sight seein'."

I looked down at my knitting then back at him. It's pretty obvious Fiona is behind the invitation, but I won't cut off my nose to spite my face.

"I'd like that."

———

FOR THE SECOND time in as many days, I found myself in the passenger seat of Conor Doherty's car. After looking over the list of places the people at the Dublin bed and breakfast had suggested I visit, we decided to go to Fair Head.

"Thank you for doing this," I said, as we merged onto the highway. "I know your mom bullied you into it."

"I wouldn't say that."

"What would you say?"

"Ma called and said you were knittin' with the ladies but would probably rather be explorin' the country on this grand day. So I volunteered ta be yer escort."

I let out a sharp chuckle. "It's probably more like you were volun-told."

The sound of his laughter made my stomach twist and flutter like I'm on a roller coaster.

"I never heard that one before." He glanced over at me, a smile lighting his face. "Mind if I use it?"

"Not at all."

"But seriously, I'm happy ta be here."

"As upset that I am about my rental car situation, having you drive works out much better for me."

"Why's that?"

"Because I get to look around at the scenery while you stay focused on the road."

I'd had enough trouble keeping my attention off my surroundings when it was gray and raining. Today with the sun shining and the sky a perfect blue, everything looks that much more spectacular.

"Glad ta be of service."

We drove in comfortable silence the rest of the way and I split my attention between the amazing view outside the car and the man sitting next to me. Both intrigued me enough that the hour-long drive flew by and before I knew it, we were turning off the main causeway and onto a smaller road.

Once we pulled onto the long, narrow drive leading down to Murlough Bay, I was even more grateful Conor was behind the wheel instead of me. I never would have navigated the steep slope and tight bends with such confidence. Plus, if I was driving, I wouldn't have been able to enjoy the gorgeous views and the sight of the mama sheep and their babies in the fields surrounding the road.

"I'm gonna park at the first stop," Conor said. "I don't wanna run into another car on its way up."

We got out of the car and stretched our legs, then he put money in the box for parking. He directed my attention to the trailhead panel, which outlined the different route choices.

"I figured we'd take the shorter loop since we're gettin' a late start."

"That sounds like a good plan."

We made our way through farmland and I was grateful I hadn't tried to do this on my own without proper shoes and clothing. The ground is uneven and soggy in places and more than once, I lost my footing. After the last time I stumbled, Conor took my hand and held it tight as we continued walking over the rugged terrain.

The initial zing I felt the first time I saw Conor has multiplied and now taken root and spread a warm attraction through my entire body. And, unless I'm reading things wrong, he shares my interest.

I have no idea how long I'll be in Ballyclare but I'd definitely like to explore whatever this is between us before I leave. Unfortunately, I'm seriously out of practice when it comes to men. Romance has taken a back seat to my career for a long time now.

That last thought made me wonder what Conor's story is. He's gorgeous, sexy as hell, and sweet. Unless the women in Ireland are blind and stupid, it's hard to believe he's totally unattached.

"Whatever yer wonderin' just ask."

"What?"

"I can hear yer brain spinning. What do ye want ta know?"

I was debating how to answer when we came to a rocky outcropping. Conor let go of my hand and followed behind me as I navigated the craggy terrain. Once we were on more even ground, he took it again, weaving our fingers together this time.

Conor's question hung in the air and I decided to answer honestly.

"I was just wondering what your story is. Are you seeing someone?"

"No."

"That's it? Just no?"

He looked down at me and smiled.

"The answer is no. What else would ye have me say?"

I shrugged. "I'm just surprised."

"Why's that?"

We made it to the top and anything I may have said was stolen by the breathtaking views. Conor directed me in front of him and put his hands on my shoulders. My heart pounded, but I couldn't say if it was from the stunning scenery in front of me or the sexy man behind me.

He stepped closer, putting his front directly against my back. Leaning his cheek against the side of my head, his sexy voice vibrated against my ear as he pointed out Rathlin Island, the Antrim Coast, and Scotland in the distance.

Conor wrapped his arms around my waist, pulling me back against him. I leaned my head against his shoulder and just enjoyed the sun shining off the water, the wind blowing through my hair, and the incredible company. And just when I didn't think the moment could get any more perfect, Conor turned me in the circle of his arms and pressed his soft lips against mine.

The kiss was tentative at first, but then he nibbled at my bottom lip and placed his mouth over mine, applying a wonderful suction that nearly brought me to my knees. I wrapped my arms around his neck, melting into his hard body as our tongues met.

I matched his tongue stroke for stroke and our surroundings faded away as all my senses focused on the taste, smell, and feel of the man making love to my mouth. He tightened his hold and pulled me onto my tiptoes.

It's been a long time for me, but I *know* I've never been kissed like this before. I shifted even closer, rubbing my hard nipples against his even harder chest. If Conor didn't have his arms locked around me, I probably would have melted into a puddle at his feet.

He slowly stroked his hand up along my waist and we both groaned when he cupped my breast. Sensation zinged down to my clit when he flicked his thumb against my nipple and I leaned into him, pressing against his erection. He pushed into me once, twice, three times before shifting his hand up to tangle his fingers into my hair. Pulling back slightly, he changed the tempo of the kiss from hot and desperate to sweet and soothing.

Dragging his mouth along my cheek, he nibbled at my earlobe and pulled back just far

enough to look into my eyes. He nudged his head to the side and the corner of his mouth kicked up in a sexy smirk.

"Come on," he said. "There's more ta see."

Oh good Lord, I hope so.

IF I THOUGHT there was a charge between Conor and me before, after our kiss on the cliff, it's even more intense. I'm surprised the car didn't spontaneously combust from all the heat flowing between us.

Our joined hands rested on the console, Conor's callused thumb stroking along mine. We've been driving for nearly an hour and have barely spoken. But as we approached Ballyclare, his gravelly voice sounded over the classic rock playing on the radio.

"I was hopin' we could continue what we started on that cliff at my place," he said. "But if ye'd prefer, I'll take ye back to Ma's."

We stopped at a red light and he turned his head to look at me. His gray eyes reflected the want I'm feeling.

"I'd like to continue what we started."

"Yeah?"

I nodded and a huge smile split his face. The light turned green and the tires squealed as he flew through the intersection. Even though he's probably going twice the speed limit, the ride to his apartment seemed to take forever. When we finally pulled into the parking lot of the garage, he brought his phone to life, and with a brush of his finger, the door opened and he pulled inside.

As he closed the door behind us, he glanced at me and said, "I normally park outside, but I don't want anyone seein' my car and stoppin' by."

"Is that a common occurrence?"

He nodded. "Pretty common."

We got out of the car and he took my hand and led me to a staircase toward the back of the garage. The light was too dim to see everything, but the space seemed to be neat and organized.

Conor gestured for me to go up the stairs in front of him and reached around me to open the door once we got to the top. As I stepped inside, the light over the copper sink offered just enough illumination for me to see the tidy kitchen. He closed the door behind us and took my hand then led me across the dark living room and through an open barn-style door on the other side.

He released my hand and I heard, more than saw, the door moving on its track as he closed it. With a soft click, a wall sconce offered enough light for me to take in his bedroom.

The enormous bed in the middle of the room was covered with navy sheets and a green, maroon, and blue plaid comforter. Other than a T-shirt tossed across the arm of the chair in the corner, there's nothing out of place.

I felt Conor behind me and turned to face him. His unwavering gaze met mine and I sucked in a startled breath at the raw hunger in his eyes.

"I know I should show ye the place, maybe offer a drink, but I can barely breathe for wantin' ye." He kissed the corner of my mouth and rested his forehead against mine. "So I'm hopin' we can save that for after."

"After?"

I nibbled at my bottom lip and Conor's eyes shifted to my mouth. He flashed a sexy smile that promised all kinds of things. Dirty things. Naughty things. Things I don't want to live without for one minute more.

That last thought must have shown on my face because Conor placed his hands on either side of my face. His thumbs lightly stroked my cheeks and the innocent action sent erotic shivers down my spine.

"Are you sure?"

"I'm sure."

"Me too," he said, before crushing his mouth to mine.

We devoured each other, our lips and tongues stroking, tasting, and savoring, as we gave in to the hunger we'd kept at bay all day. Conor opened his mouth wider and deepened the kiss as he pulled me closer.

His hands moved down my body, then back up, dragging my T-shirt with them. The kiss ended just long enough for him to pull it over my head. His clever fingers opened the button on my jeans then pulled the zipper down. Sliding his hands around and down, he gripped my ass and pulled me against the ridge of his erection. Ripping his mouth from mine, he sucked in a sharp breath. The combination of that and the heated look in his eyes sent a delicious chill down my spine.

As he stepped forward, I was forced to step back until the back of my thighs rested against the bed. He shifted his hands from my ass to my hips and lifted me then set me down on the soft mattress.

With his gaze locked on mine, he untied my boots and removed them one at a time then dropped them to the floor where they landed with a dull thud. He tugged at the hem of my jeans and dragged them down my legs and gave them the same fate.

His eyes shifted down to take a lazy tour of my body.

"Yer so beautiful. Perfect." His fingertips brushed my abdomen. "Soft."

Resting his knee on the bed next to me, he leaned down to kiss my stomach, nipping at my navel before continuing upward. Through the white lace of my bra, he teased one nipple with his tongue, tantalizing, drawing it further into the moist heat of his mouth, creating a stiff peak. His hand teased my other breast, plucking at its distended nipple.

His mouth released my right breast and moved onto the left. Our eyes held as he ran his tongue around it ever so slowly, spiraling toward my nipple. His cheeks hollowed as he sucked. My back arched as I let out a long, low moan.

"Conor." His name came out more as a sigh than a word.

"Hmm?" he muttered, creating delicious vibrations against my sensitized skin.

Pleasure shivered through me and I forgot what I was going to say.

He reached around, his fingers fumbling with the fastener of my bra, but the bed hindered his efforts. I arched to give him more wiggle room. It wasn't enough.

He backed away and I nearly cried as cool air brushed the flesh his warm mouth vacated. He held out his hand, urging me to sit up. I complied and he easily unhooked the bra, placing a gentle kiss on my shoulder in the process.

When he moved back, I realized he was still fully dressed. That didn't seem fair and I told him so.

"I'm just trying to pace myself," he said, flashing that adorable smile.

"Pace yourself with your shirt off."

I rested on my elbows and watched as he kneeled back

and lifted his T-shirt over his head, then threw it on the floor. The sight of Conor bare-chested was even better than I'd imagined. He's all six-pack and lean muscle with a happy trail leading down to the impressive bulge in his jeans.

Goosebumps trailed in my wake as I reached out and ran my fingertips over his stomach and chest. I leaned forward and placed a kiss just above his right nipple. Before I could do anything else, he tilted my face up and proceeded to kiss me senseless.

Pulling his mouth from mine, he nudged me back against the mattress, then nuzzled my breasts before moving up and nibbling on a particularly sensitive spot just above my collarbone. Back to my breasts where he sucked my nipples to tight, achy points before skimming his hot mouth down my stomach. He nibbled at my navel, dipping his tongue inside, making me squirm and chuckle out loud.

Conor hooked his fingers beneath the waistband of my panties then backed away just enough to pull them slowly down my legs. He then leaned forward and kissed my knee before deliberately inching his way up my leg, alternately kissing and nibbling on the way up.

When he settled between my thighs and placed an open-mouthed kiss at their juncture, I nearly jumped off the bed. Conor laid a restraining hand on my belly as his hot gaze met mine over the expanse of my body. He continued his sensual torture, licking and nipping and sucking until I didn't think I could take anymore. When his tongue slid over the tiny nub of nerves, I tangled my fingers in his hair and let out a long, low moan. He glanced up and I caught a glimpse of his devilish smile as he did it again, eliciting the same response.

He slipped his middle finger into my slick folds and began a steady in and out motion while his tongue circled my clit. I arched toward him, my breath coming in shallow pants. His index finger joined in the game and the rhythm increased, sending ripples of sensation through my entire body.

I was close, so close, but I wanted to hold off and make it last. As though he read my thoughts and was intent on making me lose my mind, he shifted and trailed a path of kisses up my stomach to my breasts, never once removing his hand from between my thighs. The man is a master of multitasking. Two fingers pumped while his thumb circled my clit. As if that weren't enough, he alternately sucked one nipple then the other in time with his talented hand.

It was too much. Way too much.

I dug my fingers into his shoulders and arched my back. My senses swirled as all the pleasure concentrated in that magic spot then burst through my entire body.

Cool air swept across my sweaty body as Conor moved back and removed his jeans and underwear in one swipe.

"Oh wow."

I'd said the same thing when I first saw him at Kelly's Pub, but now I'm even more speechless. The man is truly magnificent.

The corner of his mouth kicked up at my words, but the smile looked strained. I can't even imagine how he's feeling. Even after that amazing orgasm, I'm still on edge and want more.

His penis bobbed against his stomach as he leaned forward and retrieved a foil packet from the bedside table. I watched as he ripped it open and rolled the condom down his spectacular length.

My heartbeat had barely returned to normal when Conor moved between my legs and plunged inside. He pumped in and out, and I lifted my hips to meet his every thrust.

"Ruby," he said, his voice a mere rasp in my ear.

I groaned in response as I dug my fingers into his muscular ass. He picked up the pace, giving us both what we needed and I got sucked into a vortex of sensation. Wanting to feel more, needing to feel more, I shifted my hands up his back and wrapped my legs around his waist.

That did it.

I let out a long, hoarse moan as I came for the second time in less than five minutes. Some part of my brain registered the fact that Conor had let out his own shout just before he collapsed on top of me.

Chapter Eleven

I WOKE SLOWLY, snug in Conor's arms, my head resting on his chest, his heart beating slow and steady beneath my ear. Shifting just my eyes, I looked over at the clock on the nightstand and was both surprised and happy to find it's only ten-thirty.

"What're ye smilin' at?"

Conor's sleep-sexy voice sounded just above my head. Tilting it back, I met his gray eyes.

"The time."

"The time?"

I nodded. "I thought it was closer to dawn, but it's not even midnight."

"And that made ye smile?"

"It did." He kissed my forehead and I snuggled my head back against his chest. "I'm really comfortable in this gigantic bed."

His chuckle vibrated through my ear. "It's a super king, not even as long as a California king in the U.S."

"Whatever it is, it's really comfortable. Not too soft and not too firm. Just right.

Although it could be my perfect pillow." I rubbed my cheek back and forth against his chest. "I'm just happy I don't have to leave yet."

He rubbed his hand up and down my back then rested it on my hip.

"Ye don't have to leave at all."

I leaned back to look at him, resting on my elbow.

"I'm staying at your mom's house. I can't just stay out all night."

"Sure ye can. I'll just call and let her know."

Conor and I are both adults, but I'd still feel strange doing that. Plus, I'm not sure I want to announce to his family, and I imagine by default the whole town, that we spent the night together.

"And your mom would be okay with that?"

He rolled onto his side, his next words echoing my thoughts.

"We're both adults and she's just lendin' ye a room, not running a nunnery over there." My stomach flipped at his sweet smile. "Besides, she's probably home right now sayin' a rosary that we get together."

"I seriously doubt your mother is saying a rosary so we have sex."

"Never underestimate her," he said with a smirk. "Besides there had to be some divine intervention involved ta get ye in my bed. I'm not that lucky." Before I could react to his words, he said, "But I don't wanna talk about Ma or the Lord right now."

Reaching out, he wrapped his hands around my waist and pulled me in for a quick kiss. At least the first kiss was quick. The second was long, slow, deep, and wet.

I've always been a big fan of kissing and most of the men I dated never got it quite right and only seemed to treat it as a means to an end. But Conor is truly a master and seems to enjoy it as much as I do.

Even though Conor's erection poked against my stomach, he didn't try to take it to the next level. He just continued to feast on my mouth, pouring all his want and need into that kiss, and I gave all mine to him. On and on it went until we needed to pull apart to take in some air.

CONOR RELEASED my mouth and we each sucked in a deep breath before he rolled me onto my back and settled between my thighs. I felt him large and hard against me. A small shift of his hips and he'd be lined right up and could thrust right into me.

He kissed my chin, then nibbled his way along my jaw and down my neck then licked at the pulse pounding at its base before making his way downward. I settled back against the pillow enjoying every single stroke of his tongue when I remembered that I hadn't gotten to play last time. I curled my fingers into his hair and directed his attention up to my face.

"I think it's my turn to explore."

A slow smile spread across his face then he rolled off me and leaned back against his pillows and spread his arms out before tucking them beneath his head.

"I'm all yers."

———

CONOR PULLED INTO HIS PARENTS' driveway and circled around to the front. It's just past midnight but there's still a soft glow in the first-floor windows. After shifting the car into park, he turned to face me and leaned his arm on the back of my seat.

"Thank you so much for today," I said. "I had an amazing time."

"Yer very welcome."

"I definitely want to go back to Fair Head and do the longer trail. It was so beautiful there. I'm surprised there weren't more people. The day was perfect."

"The tourist buses don't go there, so it never gets too crowded. Not like some of the other places."

"Good to know."

"And so ye know, while yer here, I'd be happy ta accompany ye again wherever ye'd like ta go."

I nibbled at my bottom lip and looked down at my lap before meeting his gaze again.

"I'd like that."

A slow smile spread across his face and he rested his forehead against mine.

"And just so ye know. I enjoyed everythin' that happened after Fair Head, too."

He kissed me softly then pulled back.

"So did I."

"Maybe we can do that again sometime, too."

"I'd definitely like that," I said.

I saw something out of the corner of my eye at the house and I turned my head to get a better look. Conor followed my gaze then looked back at me.

"What's wrong?" he asked.

"I don't know. Nothing I guess. Something caught my eye, but I have no idea what and I don't see anything now."

He smirked. "I'm guessin' it was Ma lookin' out the window. Ye probably saw the curtain move."

"You think she's waiting up for me?"

"Old habits. She never went ta sleep before we were all home."

"If I knew that, I would have had you take me home earlier. I hate the thought of keeping her awake."

"She doesn't sleep much anyway." He sat straight and opened his car door. "Let's go on the porch so I can kiss ye goodnight properly without her watchin'."

He got out and jogged around the front of the car and opened my door then took my hand and helped me out. He didn't let go as we walked to the porch and up the three steps that brought us to the front door.

Turning to face me, Conor placed his hands on either side of my face and looked into my eyes.

"I had a great time today, Ruby. Thank you."

He leaned down and gave me a "proper" kiss, which was more than a little bit improper. Especially considering the fact we're standing on his parents' front porch with his mother probably trying her best to peek out the window at us.

He gave me one final soft peck then stepped back.

"Good night, Ruby Devlin. I'll see ye tomorrow at breakfast and we'll head out for the day."

"Sounds good."

I smiled and waved then watched him walk back to the car, get behind the wheel, and drive away. Twisting the knob, I opened the door and stepped into the house. I'd just reached the stairs when Fiona emerged from the kitchen.

"Oh Ruby, I thought I heard the door," she said innocently, as if she hadn't been spying on Conor and me minutes ago. "Did ye have a good time?"

"It was spectacular."

"That's good ta hear."

The knowing smirk on her face should have made me uncomfortable but the day...and night...had been too amazing for me to feel anything but happy.

Chapter Twelve

FOR SOMEONE who considered a bagel and coffee a large breakfast for the past decade, after just three days, I was used to Fiona's morning feasts. In fact, I woke with my stomach growling, and by the time I showered and got dressed, I was ravenous. Of course, that could have something to do with all the energy I expended yesterday, especially last night.

That last thought made me move down the stairs faster in anticipation of seeing Conor. As I entered the kitchen and looked around, I was disappointed when he wasn't there.

"Mrs. O'Leary's car broke down early this mornin' and Conor is fixin' it." Fiona patted my back as she passed behind me then settled into her usual chair. "He said ta tell ye he'll be here as soon as he's through."

"Okay. Thanks."

I sat, immediately filled my plate, and dug in. As I chewed, I realized that the normally loud table had gotten totally quiet and looked up. Brady, Ronan, and Mac were hyper-focused on their plates and Fiona watched me, a smile on her face. The only one acting normal was Paddy, who read his paper while he ate.

Obviously Fiona shared the fact that Conor and I did more than sightsee yesterday. My initial reaction to that was embarrassment, but I know that's just leftover programming from my Catholic upbringing. Gran was cool for her generation, but sex was never discussed in our house, which always made it seem taboo. When I moved out, the men I spent time with were as focused on their careers as I was and I never met their families. So this is all new.

"So where did ye visit yesterday?" Fiona asked.

"Fair Head."

"Oh, it's lovely there."

"It really is and the weather was so beautiful."

"Where're the two of ye headed today?" Ronan asked.

"I'm not sure." Glancing out at the gray skies, I added, "It doesn't look quite so perfect out there today."

Mac's phone dinged and he checked it. After muttering a curse, he shoved his last bite of food into his mouth, chewed, and swallowed.

"Ma, that thing I told ye about needs ta be fixed. I'm gonna go work in the office."

He picked up his computer bag then stood, nodded at me, and left the room.

"I hope everything is okay," I said.

Fiona shrugged. "I don't pretend ta know what he does on that computer, but I do know

he has a client that's bein' fussy."

"He's upgradin' a site for a big client and they're not thrilled with the graphics," Brady said.

"He needs ta hire someone ta do that," Ronan added, then looked at me and explained. "His ex-fiancée used ta work with him doing the artsy stuff, but since they broke up last year, he's been doin' it all and it's not his thing."

I spread blackberry jam on the last bite of my toast then popped it into my mouth.

"Well, at one time it was *my* thing. Do you think he'd welcome my help?"

"Couldn't hurt ta ask," Brady said.

I stood and picked up my plate.

"Don't ye fuss now," Fiona said, resting her hand on my wrist.

"It was part of our deal when you offered to let me stay here, remember? I'll put this in the sink and go see if I can help Mac, then I'll be back to load the dishwasher."

Before Fiona could argue, I walked across the room, dropped my dish in the sink, and headed to the office.

I found Mac sitting behind the desk, frowning at the computer monitor. He glanced up when he heard me enter.

"Brady mentioned your issue and I was wondering if I could help. I used to regularly create graphics."

He leaned back in the chair and shrugged.

"I can code anythin' but the graphics drive me nuts."

I walked around the desk and looked down at his screen.

"What are you trying to do?"

Sitting forward again, he clicked on the mouse, moving the cursor over four different pictures on his laptop screen.

"They want that lady, ground, sky, and sun, and want their brand colors incorporated," he said, then directed my attention to the big monitor. "That's what I made, but they don't like it and I can't say I blame them."

"It's not horrible, you just need to blend the edges better, maybe resize and reposition a couple things. And I'd use their colors differently." I looked down at him. "Do you mind if I give it a try?"

Mac stood and gestured toward the desk chair. I sat and saved a copy of his version, then went to work. He pulled over a chair and sat next to me, then rested his elbow against the desk, his eyes glued to the screen. I expected him to ask questions or give direction, but he just watched.

The front door opened and out of the corner of my eye, I saw Conor enter and pass the doorway, then reappear.

"What's goin' on in here?" he asked as he walked into the office.

"Mac was having some trouble with graphics and I volunteered to help."

"Aren't ye supposed ta be on vacation?"

My stomach flipped at his teasing smile and I wondered if he'd consider spending the day at his place and exploring each other some more instead of the country. He must have read my thoughts because that smile turned less teasing and more knowing.

"Something like that," I said, breaking the spell before we spontaneously combusted. "But it doesn't mean I can't help out."

"Well, I'll be in the kitchen when yer done."

After one last hot glance, he rapped his knuckles on the doorframe and left the room.

I stared at the empty space for a few seconds before blinking and returning my attention to the computer screen. It took me a minute to get his sexy image out of my head so I could focus on what I was doing before he'd appeared, which in itself is a first. No man has ever distracted me from work, which probably explains why none of my relationships ever lasted.

"Did they say if they want one of their brand colors to be dominant?" I asked once I was satisfied with the graphic.

When he didn't answer, I glanced over at Mac and found him staring at me instead of looking at the screen.

"He likes ye." I blinked at his unexpected words. "Conor," he added.

"Oh. Well, I like him too."

More than I should considering we've only known each other a few days. But despite that fact, there's just something between us that I've never felt before.

"I know yer bein' here is temporary and so does he, but like I said, he likes ye so logic might not apply. He doesn't bring everyone he tows home to stay with Ma, ye know. So just keep that in mind."

His eyes are so similar to Conor's, but I don't feel a thing as I look into them. Other than envious that Conor has someone care enough about him that he'd start this awkward conversation.

The funny thing is, once I leave and this thing between Conor and me is over...whatever *this* is...he'll still be living in his hometown surrounded by his whole family and I'll be alone wherever I happen to find a job. So he'll probably be better off than me.

Still, I nodded and said, "I will."

Chapter Thirteen

I STRETCHED OUT MY ARM, trying to calm the pins and needles that had woken me without disturbing Conor. He was up so early, then we'd had a full day so I'm sure he's exhausted. It's only nine o'clock so I can let him sleep a couple more hours before I wake him to take me back to his parents' house.

Bending my elbow, I wiggled my fingers, then settled them against his hair and slowly ran them through the soft strands. He let out a soft sigh and snuggled his cheek against me.

"Mmm, that feels nice," he said in a sleepy voice.

"Sorry, I didn't mean to wake you."

"No worries." He kissed my shoulder. "I'm kinda embarrassed that I'm sleepin' instead a takin' advantage of the fact that I have a beautiful woman in my bed." Wrapping his arm around my waist, he squeezed me tight. "But this is too nice."

I hummed my agreement.

"Speaking of nice, thank you for today. I had a great time."

"It would'a been better if it didn't rain all day."

He took me to the Giant's Causeway, and even though the day was wet and drizzly, the views were absolutely stunning. We walked down the pathway, but in deference to the weather, didn't venture onto the stones.

"Oh that was just a wee mist," I said, mimicking his words from earlier.

My laughter echoed through the room when he tickled my stomach then rolled me onto my back.

"Are ye mockin' me?"

"Never," I said with a big smile.

He gave me a quick kiss then rested his head on the pillow next to me. I looked around the room then shifted onto my side to face him.

"Did ye sleep at all or were ye starin' at the ceilin' after I conked out?"

I nodded. "Don't forget, I drank a *lot* of whiskey. I only woke because my arm fell asleep."

After we left The Causeway, we stopped for a quick dinner before going to the Old Bushmills Distillery for a tour and tasting. Since he was driving, Conor limited himself, but I sampled everything they poured.

"Ye seemed ta enjoy it."

"Every single drop was delicious."

"I saw ye were drinkin' Bushmills at Kelly's when I came ta tow ye. So I figured ye'd enjoy goin' there."

"I'm impressed you noticed that."

"It caught my attention. Most Americans who come here are more familiar with Jameson. That's the case at my brother's pub anyway."

"Bushmills was Gran's favorite so it's what I grew up seeing."

As usual, thoughts of my grandmother gave me a bittersweet ache right in the center of my chest. My eyes still fill with tears whenever I think about her. So instead of dampening the mood, I changed the subject.

"I really like your place. It's so cozy," I said. "Especially this bed."

He looked around the room.

"Up here was used fer storage but when I moved back and started workin' at the garage, Ronan, Brady, and Mac helped me remodel."

"Moved back?" He nodded. "From where?"

"Dublin."

"How long did you live there?"

"About seven years."

"What did you do there?"

"Investment bankin'."

My eyes widened. "Really?"

"Is that so surprisin'?" he asked around a chuckle.

"It is," I said, then quickly added, "And I don't mean that to be insulting. It's just that I can't picture you living anywhere but here, never mind sitting in a stuffy office all day."

"I'm guessin' ye'd know somethin' about stuffy offices."

"My last few weren't so bad, but some were barely closets. But even they were better than sitting in a cube farm."

"I agree with ye there."

"So you were in Dublin, working as an investment banker. How did you end up back in Ballyclare owning a garage?"

He shrugged. "My gran died and I came back for the funeral and stayed a couple weeks. When I went back, somethin' was different. I didn't like my job anymore and the city was too loud."

"So you just moved back?"

"Not right away. I gave it about six months ta see if I'd settle in again, but I didn't. I just got more miserable." He took in a deep breath and let it out. "I was livin' with someone at the time so I really tried, but I just didn't want ta be there anymore."

"Since she's not here, I'm guessing she chose to stay there."

"You win the prize," he said with a sad smile. "It wasn't her fault. I'm the one who changed what I wanted."

"And what was that?"

"I always wanted ta live in a big city and have a desk job with regular hours. But then when I came back here for that funeral, I realized I missed my family and I enjoyed workin' at the house or here more than sittin' behind my desk. My Da was lookin' ta cut back his hours so the timin' was right."

"And the woman?"

"Neither one of us was too broken up when I left so that tells its own story."

"Have you ever regretted it?"

"Not one second of one day," he said without pause. "Ye might'a noticed my family is close." I nodded. "After Gran died, it made me think that someday Ma and Da won't be here anymore so I should spend time with them while I can. If I was livin' my dream, it would'a been different, but I wasn't. Not after the funeral anyway."

His words make me wonder what I would have done if I'd had that epiphany while Gran was still alive. Would I have quit my job and moved home? Chances are I wouldn't have. I had such tunnel vision, I'm not sure anything would have strayed me from my course.

And that wasted time is something I'll just have to live with.

Chapter Fourteen

CONOR and I got an early start today and managed to explore Derry and Donegal before driving down to Belleek. There we took the pottery tour and visited the museum before heading back to Ballyclare and Brady's bar...which is also called Brady's...where apparently the fact that it's Saturday night is cause for a celebration. The parking lot was jammed and we ended up parking down the road a bit and walking.

As Conor opened the door, we were faced with a wall of people. He took my hand and parted the crowd, leading me toward the bar. People stopped him every few steps to say hello and he introduced me along the way as we made our way further into the room. Conor stopped at the edge of the bar and pulled me forward to stand next to him.

"Granda."

The man sitting at the corner had been talking to the man next to him but swiveled around to face us.

"Conor, glad ta see ye." His gray eyes shifted to me. "And ye must be the gal's been keepin' Conor busy."

"Granda, this is Ruby Devlin. Ruby, this is Niall Brady, Ma's da."

His grandfather took my hand and placed a kiss on the back of it.

"It's nice ta meet ye, Ruby Devlin. Yer absolutely lovely." He looked over his shoulder at the man he'd been talking to, who he introduced as Steven Lyons. "Doesn't she look like that girl?"

"What girl?" Steven asked.

"Ye know, the actress. The one from that movie. The one set in Ireland."

"Catherine O'Hara?"

"Lord no," Niall said. "The one with the strawberry hair. She had the suitcase and was tryin' ta get ta Dublin."

Both men stared at me and I glanced at Conor who was watching me with a frown. Then his eyes widened.

"*Leap Year*. The movie was *Leap Year*. I don' remember the actress, though." Snapping his fingers, he looked up at the ceiling then back at me and smiled. "Amy Adams." His eyes shifted to Niall. "She does look like her. I didn't notice before."

Amy Adams?

I won't complain about that.

"It's nice to meet you too, Mr. Brady," I said.

"You call me Niall," he said. Then added with a wink, "Or Granda."

Brady pushed two pints toward us before I had to respond to that.

"Thank you," I said as I picked mine up and took a long drink.

"Yer welcome."

"Good crowd tonight," Conor said.

Brady nodded and looked around the room.

"The Leftovers are playin'. They're always a favorite."

His last couple of words were drowned out by the cheering crowd when the band stepped onto the make-shift stage.

"That's my cue ta leave," Niall said and both he and Steve stood. "Ruby, ye can have my stool. It's the best one in the place." Taking my hand, he ushered me to the spot he'd just vacated then kissed me on the cheek. "Will I see ye at church tomorrow?"

"Oh uh." My eyes shifted to Conor.

Niall's hearty laugh brought my attention back to him.

"Didn't mean ta put ye on the spot there," he said. "If I don't see ye at mass, I'll see ye at breakfast after."

"Great. I'll see you then."

He gave Conor a hearty hug then the two men disappeared into the crowd.

"He seems sweet," I said.

Conor nodded and I swiveled to look at him as he slid into the seat next to me.

"He's havin' a hard time adjustin' ta retirement." He took a sip of his Guinness. "He ran this place for a long time and just turned it over ta Brady a couple years ago. Gran pretty much made him after he had a mild stroke. So now he comes and hangs out. Until the music starts, that is."

I turned my attention to the other end of the room when the lead singer introduced the band and they started to play.

"What?" Conor said from right beside my ear so I could hear him.

"Nothing." I shrugged. "I just wasn't expecting Bon Jovi."

"What *were* ye expectin'?"

"Not *Livin' On a Prayer.* Something by U2 or Van Morrison," I added with a chuckle. "Or maybe *Wild Mountain Thyme* if we're in the mood for a sing-along."

"Sorry ta disappoint." He touched his lips to mine then pulled back just far enough to look into my eyes. "We can leave whenever yer ready, but I wanted ta stop by and show ye the place.

"No, this is fun." I rested my hand on his cheek and leaned in for a lingering kiss.

He pulled back and looked over my shoulder then frowned. "Perfect timin' as always."

I turned around.

"Oh hey," I said to Ronan and Mac and spun my chair to fully face them.

Ronan looked at me then shifted his eyes between his brothers.

"Granda is right. Ruby does look like Amy Adams. Can't believe he noticed it before us."

"I'm guessin' you ran into him in the parking lot," Conor said.

Mac nodded and walked behind the bar. He poured two drafts then came back and handed one to Ronan before holding up his beer in my direction.

"I owe ye," he said. "My client loved the graphics ye did. Ye saved my arse."

"Oh, I'm so happy they liked them," I said. "It's good to know I haven't lost my touch."

"Definitely not," he said.

He started to say something else, but the crowd cheered as the song ended making it louder than when the music was playing. They settled down once the band went into the next song, *The Old Apartment* by Barenaked Ladies.

"If ye have time tomorrow, would ye be willin' ta look at a couple more things I'm workin' on?" Mac asked.

"Oh sure."

"I'm happy ta pay ye. I don't expect ye ta work fer free."

"Absolutely not. I'm happy to help."

"Well, I appreciate it. I'll bring my computer to breakfast again." He looked over at Conor. "I don't imagine it'll take too long so it shouldn't interfere with whatever plans ye've got."

"And while Ruby's busy, maybe ye can help me fix some fence and the door ta my loft. It's stickin' again," Ronan said. "Neither should take too long, but they're both two-man jobs."

Conor nodded and finished his beer.

"Seems like ye two had this planned."

"No, it just worked out," Ronan said.

"He's not lyin'. I just happen to suck at graphics and Ruby is a pro. It's divine intervention she ended up here."

I've had that same thought more than once, but didn't say so.

"You don't suck," I said. "You just need to learn how to fine-tune things. I can show you a few tricks that'll help."

"Or maybe we can talk about ye joinin' me," Mac said. "I need ta hire someone ta do graphics and yer in need of a job."

I wasn't not sure if he's serious or not, but before I had to respond, the band switched to *Wonderful* by Everclear and Mac put his fingers up to his mouth and whistled.

"I *love* this song," he said, then sang along, effectively putting an end to the conversation.

I turned my attention to the band too, but it didn't stop me from turning his words over in my head.

Chapter Fifteen

I QUIETLY ATE MY BREAKFAST, observing the crowd around me. Aside from Conor's brothers and grandparents, several aunts, uncles, and cousins came back to the house after church for breakfast. Well, I suppose it's actually more of a brunch and Fiona has gone all out.

Instead of eating in the kitchen, we're in the formal dining room. The bulk of the food is set buffet-style on the server, with a variety of breads, danishes, and pastries spread out across the table. Her usual breakfasts are pretty spectacular, but this is nothing less than a feast.

"Yer awful quiet," Conor said.

I looked over at him and smiled.

"I'm just amazed at the amount of food and all the people. Does your mom really do this every week?"

"Sometimes one of my aunts hosts, but usually it's Ma because there's more space here. Plus, she's a better cook," he added with a wink.

A sense of melancholy rolled through me as I looked around the room again. It's a feeling I've been fighting to keep at bay since I accompanied the family to church earlier. . I can't even imagine what it's like to grow up surrounded by so many people.

The only person I could ever count on was Gran and now that she's gone, it's just me. I've had a multitude of friends through the years, but all those relationships were more superficial than anything. And as I moved up the corporate ladder, the number of women I hung around with socially decreased significantly.

"I'm goin' out ta the barn," Ronan said.

I'd been so in my head, I didn't even notice he'd approached.

"I'll be out in a couple," Conor said then turned to me when Ronan left the room. "Are you sure there's nothin' wrong?"

I looked at him, a forced smile on my face.

"I'm sure."

Serious gray eyes studied my face. He still didn't look convinced but didn't push.

"I shouldn't be too long with Ronan. The sooner I go, the sooner I'll be done," he said after we both cleared our plates. "Are ye finished?" he asked. When I nodded, he took my plate and put it on top of his. Leaning over, he kissed me. "I'll come find ye when I'm done."

That said, he picked up both plates and stood, then walked toward the kitchen.

I chatted with his aunts and a couple of his cousins, then excused myself to go find Mac. Like Conor said, the sooner we get started, the sooner we'll get done and we can go explore. I bumped into Mac in the hallway and we both walked to the office.

"There are four graphics, all for the same client." He powered up his computer and connected it to the large monitor so we have two screens to work with.

I sat in the desk chair and Mac pulled up a seat next to me just like last time.

"I tried to touch them up usin' what ye showed me, but they still didn't turn out as nice."

"It takes practice," I said. "You'll get the hang of it."

"That seems unlikely."

Loud laughter floated from the dining room and I glanced over at Mac.

"You can go hang with your family if you want. I'll call you when I'm done."

"If ye don't mind, I'd like ta stay and watch."

"I don't mind at all."

I turned my attention back to the first graphic and tightened it up with a few clicks of the mouse. The second needed a little more work.

"Do you have the original image you're using in this?" He reached for the mouse and opened a file then brought it up. "If you use this part of the image and turn it like this, it will work better."

"Why didn't I see that?"

"A lot of this is just practice and experience," I said.

"And the rest is an artsy side I just don't have."

"All this can be learned."

He shook his head.

"The computer stuff can but the design is somethin' ye either have or ye don't."

"Not necessarily."

I fixed and saved the third picture and moved on to the fourth. Again I needed to change the portion of the image used, but it still only took a few minutes to fix. Once I was done, I saved my work and sat back in the chair.

"Anything else you want me to look at?"

Mac shook his head.

"Ye know Ruby, I was only half-kiddin' when I offered

ye a job last night," he said. "I know you were a CEO of a huge company and my little job probably sounds like an insult, but things are growin' here. It'll never be MODCO, but I think we'd do well," he said. "Bailey...that's my ex...did a good job marketin' and we got a good start. Then word a mouth kicked in so now I have more than I can handle."

"Do you have anyone helping you?"

"A couple regular freelancers for the coding and my cousin Holly helps with the books, but no one full-time." He sat back and dragged his fingers through his hair. "I know ye bought a one-way ticket here so I dunno when ye plan on goin' home, but we could work somethin' out if yer interested."

Home.

With Gran gone, I don't even know where that is anymore. My throat tightened and I looked back at the monitor to hide the fact that I'm blinking back tears.

"I'll definitely think about it."

Mac didn't comment on my thick, wobbly voice. He also didn't stop me when I ran out of the office without another word.

Chapter Sixteen

THANKFULLY I DIDN'T SEE anyone as I ran out of the house. I didn't have a destination in mind, but I made sure to go in the opposite direction of the barn. I didn't want to see Conor when I'm feeling so raw.

I slowed to a walk and swiped at the tears streaming down my cheeks. The terrain was getting bumpier and more overgrown and I didn't want to fall and break something.

Through blurry eyes, I spotted the pond and headed in that direction. In the peaceful quiet, my footsteps sounded loud on the dock. I walked to the edge and sat, my feet dangling over the water.

Sobs wracked my body as regret, thick and all-consuming, devoured me. It's a horrible feeling, knowing I wasted more than a decade of my life chasing a career that just didn't matter while ignoring the one person who did. I traded time with Gran and meaningful relationships for empty work connections and steps up the corporate ladder.

And for what?

My full bank account and impressive resume don't

make up for the fact that with Gran gone, I'm truly alone in this world. I don't even have anyone close enough to list as my *In Case of Emergency* contact. That's pretty pathetic.

Leaning my head against the railing, I stared out at the water, watching the little ripples created by the breeze. Every once in a while the sun peeked through the clouds, making those tiny waves glimmer and gleam and I focused on that sight as I fought to get myself under control.

My tears slowed and I sniffed, feeling weighed down with an all-consuming regret. Using the sleeve of my shirt, I dried my cheeks and wiped under my nose. I wanted to scream and let it all out, but I knew that wouldn't do any good. It would only make my throat more raw and hurt my head.

"Ruby?"

I stiffened at the sound of Conor's voice. I'd been so lost in my misery, I didn't even hear him approach. The dock shook and soon his reflection appeared in the water just over mine.

"Are ye all right?" I nodded, not trusting myself to speak. "Can I join ye?"

I nodded again and felt his shoulder bump against mine as he sat. Without saying a word, he wrapped his arm around my waist. The kind gesture made my tears flow again and I rested my head against his shoulder as I bawled my eyes out.

When the storm passed, he kissed the top of my head.

"Wanna talk about it?"

That's a complicated question. Or I guess just the answer is.

"I don't know," I said. "As ridiculous as it sounds, spending time with your family today made me realize how alone I am now that Gran's gone."

Conor didn't comment. He just held me tight, his

cheek resting against my head as he waited for me to speak again.

"I should have been with her instead of moving all over the country chasing promotions. And for what? It's not like the company gave me the same loyalty. They showed me how expendable I was when they let me go." I shifted back and looked up at him. "Gran is what really mattered and I treated her like an afterthought. Like we had all the time in the world. Like she'd always be there when I was feeling generous enough to spend time with her. How could I have ignored her like that?"

"It doesn't sound ta me like ye ignored her as much as ye lived yer life," he said. "Those are two different things."

"Well, I wasn't with her."

"Did ye talk ta her regularly?"

I nodded. "We talked all the time and I bought her an iPhone so we could FaceTime."

He shifted back and placed his hands on either side of my face and used his thumbs to wipe the tears from my cheeks.

"So ye didn't ignore her."

"It wasn't the same as being with her and I was all she had." I hiccuped. "I'd give anything to get back that time."

"I know."

He shifted sideways and leaned back against the railing then pulled me between his legs so I could rest my head against his chest. I wrapped my arms around his waist and listened to the steady beat of his heart as his hand moved up and down my back in long, comforting strokes.

I have no idea how long we sat like that, but eventually my tears subsided and the ache in my chest receded enough so I could breathe normally.

"How about if we bypass my family and go back ta my apartment?"

"Are you sure?"

"We were leavin' ta go sightseein' anyway."

His eyes skimmed over my face as he waited for my response and I cringed. I can't imagine what I look like after my mini-meltdown.

"Okay." I sniffed. "Thank you, Conor."

"No need fer thanks."

He stood and held his hand out to help me up and continued to hold it as we walked off the dock and toward the house. His car was parked at the end of the driveway and thankfully no one blocked him in. After opening the passenger door, Conor stepped back and waited for me to get settled into the seat before closing it. I watched him walk around the front of the car and as he opened his door, he looked back at the house.

Leaning down, he said, "Ma has yer phone. I'll be right back."

He jogged toward the porch and Fiona met him at the bottom of the steps and handed him my phone. She said something then glanced toward the car, looking concerned, as Conor responded. He shook his head and said something else. She hugged him then stepped back and watched as he made his way back to the car.

Without saying a word, he handed me my phone then started the car and pulled onto the road. I looked down and saw five missed calls and three texts from him. I'm not sure how he found me, but I'm glad he did. Just having him near made me feel better.

Minutes later, he turned into his parking lot and pulled into the garage. After we got out of the car, he rested his hand on the small of my back as we walked upstairs to his apartment. I followed him into the bedroom and watched as he opened a drawer and pulled out a T-shirt.

"I figured ye'd want ta get comfortable," he said. "I'm gonna go get us some drinks."

I changed into his shirt and placed my folded clothes on top of the dresser. He walked back into the room carrying two glasses of water in one hand and one glass of whiskey in the other.

"I wasn't sure which ye'd prefer, so I brought both."

I reached for the whiskey and took two quick sips, welcoming the calming warmth it spread through my body. Conor settled onto the other side of the bed and gestured for me to join him.

After finishing the whiskey, I placed the glass on the nightstand then picked up the water Conor had set there. I drank half of it in one long gulp before climbing in next to him and resting my head against his chest.

He wrapped his arm around my shoulders and pulled me closer as his other hand pointed the remote toward the TV and turned it on. I closed my eyes as he searched for something to watch.

"Since Granda mentioned this last night, I figured it'd be fun ta watch together." I opened my eyes and smiled as the opening scene of *Leap Year* filled the screen.

"Sounds perfect."

Chapter Seventeen

I WOKE to the sound of my phone ringing. After peeling myself off Conor, I rolled over and grabbed it from the nightstand.

"Hello?"

"Ruby Devlin?"

I cleared my throat. "Yes."

"This is Lara Black calling about your rental car."

"Oh hi."

I sat and pushed my hair away from my face.

"We have a new car for you and can deliver it and pick the other up. I just need an address."

"That's great. Hold on." I looked at Conor. "What's the address here?" He told me and I recited it to her.

"Perfect," she said. "They'll be there between two and four today."

"I appreciate it."

"And I appreciate your patience. Is there anything else I can help you with?"

"No, I'm good. Thank you for your help."

I ended the call and rested my phone in my lap.

"So yer new car is comin'?"

"Yeah."

"Now what?"

"What do you mean?"

"Where will ye go?"

"I don't know." I let out a nervous laugh. "I mean, this whole trip has been unplanned so I'm not really sure."

He nodded and looked like he was going to say something, but rolled over and sat on the edge of the bed instead.

"Are ye hungry?"

"I am," I said around a chuckle.

"What's so funny about that?"

"I was never really a breakfast eater, but since staying with your mom, I wake up starving."

"Maybe it's the different air."

"Whatever it is, the answer is yes. I'm very hungry."

"Come on then. Let's go cook somethin'."

I followed him into the kitchen and helped the best I could, which basically consisted of making toast. With not much else to do, I was able to observe Conor as he cooked eggs and sausage, his boxers riding low on his hips.

Physically, the man's a solid twenty on a scale of one to ten. Add in his personality, how sweet he is, and the fact that he can cook and he's even more off the charts. I consider myself fortunate that I crashed in Ballyclare and he's the one who came to tow me. The time I've spent in Ireland would have been totally different without him. Definitely less enjoyable.

He turned off the stove, split the food between two plates, and carried them over to the table. I followed with the toast and sat in the chair he'd pulled out for me.

After I praised his culinary skills, we ate in silence until our plates were nearly empty.

"I want to thank you for yesterday," I finally said.

"Ye don't need ta thank me."

"Maybe not, but I'm going to. I was a mess and you were amazing."

"Ye went through a lot before ye came here. All those feelings have ta come out sometime."

"I guess so, but in the middle of your family's after-church gathering wasn't ideal timing. I barely made it out of the house before I lost it. Poor Mac must think I'm nuts. Not to mention your mother."

"Mac thinks nothin' of the sort. Neither does Ma." He took a bite of toast and continued after he swallowed. "She was worried about ye though."

His words caused an ache in my chest, but it's different than the one that was there yesterday. This was more of a longing for what's missing in my life than despair over all the time I missed with Gran.

"Did you tell her what was wrong?"

"No. She figured it was about your Gran though."

"And Mac?"

"Same thing. He texted last night after ye fell asleep ta make sure ye were okay."

I picked up my napkin and wiped my hands then crumbled it and placed it on my empty plate.

"Your family is amazing. You're very lucky."

He nodded. "I know it."

"If we'd met a few months ago and you'd told me you gave up your career and moved back here, I would have thought you were crazy. But now I totally understand."

I stood and picked up both of our dishes and carried them to the sink.

"I can do that," Conor said from directly behind me.

"You cooked, I'll clean."

As I turned on the water, he moved over and leaned his hip against the counter. His bulging biceps and six-pack abs teased my peripheral vision and I struggled to focus on the task at hand.

"I want ta propose somethin'."

"What's that?"

I soaped up one dish, rinsed it off, and set it in the drying rack.

"What if, instead of venturin' on yer own, we explore together like we've been doin'?"

I blinked, both shocked and pleased at his words, and rinsed the second dish. After setting it next to the other one to dry, I quickly washed the pan and silverware then turned off the water.

"Don't you have to work?" I asked as I dried my hands on the towel he handed me.

He shrugged. "I'm lucky enough ta be able ta make my own schedule and if we're away and there's an emergency, Da or one of my brothers will fill in."

If I'm being totally honest, I don't want my time with Conor to come to an end. When I received that phone call about my rental, I should have been relieved, but instead my stomach twisted with dread at the thought of leaving.

"Are you sure?"

"Positive."

I draped the towel over the sink and smoothed it into place then smiled up at him.

"I'd love to stay."

"I do have ta add that there's one condition."

"What's that?"

"Ye have ta stay here with me instead of at Ma's."

He wrapped his arms around my waist and pulled me

close for a quick kiss. I looked up at him through my eyelashes and smiled.

"You drive a hard bargain, but my answer is still yes."

I missed his warmth when he stepped back, but his words heated me right up again.

"Let's go take a long, hot shower and when we come up for air, we'll go collect yer things and bring 'em here."

Chapter Eighteen

"SO WHAT WOULD ye want ta do today?"

Conor stroked his fingers up and down my arm as we relaxed, wrapped around each other in the middle of his giant bed. He'd woken me by nibbling his way along my jaw and down my neck then latching onto my left nipple. And things only got better from there.

"What's left to do? I feel like we've explored all of Northern Ireland."

"The rest of the country?"

I pinched his waist, or at least attempted to. Since he's all lean muscle, I basically just scratched my fingernails against his skin.

"The rest of the country is too far for a day trip."

"I know that." He kissed the top of my head. "That's why I was thinkin' we could maybe take a train and go west for a couple days. Rent a car and explore over there."

And that's how we ended up on a train heading to the other side of the country.

When I worked in Manhattan and lived in Brooklyn, I

took the train to work every day. But I never just enjoyed the ride. I always had my nose in my computer, working.

This time, I just sat back, looked out the window, and enjoyed the scenery. Not to mention the company. And that's the way it's been since I got here. Other than to take pictures, I've barely looked at my cell. And the only computer I've touched is Mac's.

You'd think I'd be going through some kind of tech withdrawal but it's been very liberating. This whole trip has been freeing. Eventually I'll have to go back to the real world, but I'll cross that bridge when I come to it.

"Tell me about your garage," I said, shifting to look at Conor.

"What about it?"

"You've been spending a lot of time with me. I hope your business isn't suffering."

"Yer wonderin' how I make a livin'."

"I am kind of curious."

"I own the garage free and clear so my cost of living is low." He took my hand and wrapped our fingers together. "Most of my income comes from two things, investments and restorin' and sellin' classic cars. I sold my latest about three weeks ago and haven't found a new one ta work on so I have some time on my hands."

He lifted our joined hands and kissed the back of mine then rested them on his thigh again.

"So you don't do regular garage stuff?"

"I do but usually only for my Da's old customers. I don't look fer new ones." Smiling over at me he added, "Jamie Kelly is one of my regulars. That's why he called me ta come get ye."

"And the investments?"

"Without soundin' full a myself, I'm good at it. So I've

done well." He shrugged. "It is what I used ta do fer a livin'."

"Maybe I should have you look at my portfolio," I said with a chuckle.

"I'm happy ta look at anythin' of yers."

He bobbed his eyebrows then leaned down and kissed me.

———

WE ARRIVED in County Clare and picked up the rental car Conor had booked earlier. Instead of heading out sightseeing, he suggested we go to the hotel he'd also booked, saying he had a surprise. Even though I was curious, I didn't bug for details. Not that anything he disclosed would have prepared me for the sight that greeted me as we turned into the gates and drove up the length of the wooded driveway.

"Is that a *castle*?"

"Can't put nothin' past you."

I dragged my gaze from the impressive sight in front of me and looked over at him.

"Seriously. That's an actual castle," I said. "We're staying here?"

"We are."

We pulled under the portico and were greeted by a valet. He opened my door and after I stepped out, he walked over to Conor and took the fob and handed him a ticket.

Conor grabbed our bag from the backseat and we made our way inside, which was as magnificent as the outside. The staff greeted us with smiling faces and as they checked us in, I looked around at the stunning decor, which was somehow grand and homey at the same time.

Through the years, I've stayed in some of the most lavish hotels in the United States, but none hold a candle to this. As we made our way to our room, I took in the flawless decor. Each detail in the common areas was more elegant than the next.

Our room was stylish and sophisticated, yet practical and comfortable. I peeked into the bathroom and was happy to find that it's somehow equipped with every modern convenience while still keeping its historic grandeur. My eyes drifted to the enormous claw-foot tub that's easily big enough for two.

I peeked into the bathroom and was happy to find that it's somehow equipped with every modern convenience while still keeping its historic grandeur. My eyes drifted to the enormous claw-foot tub that's easily big enough for two.

"Conor, this place is amazing," I said.

"I'm glad ye like it."

"Have you stayed here before?"

"My cousin's weddin' was here a few years ago. The whole family stayed fer a long weekend."

I chuckled. "You probably bought out the whole hotel."

"Not quite, but there was a crew of us."

He wrapped his arms around my waist and pulled me in for a kiss.

"I thought we could eat dinner here and explore the grounds, then maybe get ta bed early."

"I like every one of those ideas."

Chapter Nineteen

THE MORNING DAWNED clear and bright, a perfect day for visiting the Cliffs of Moher. And once again, I was stunned speechless. Magnificent hardly describes the beautiful rugged cliffs, the raw green of the grass, and the blue of the Atlantic Ocean. The view from every single point is absolutely spectacular.

"Conor, this is amazing."

I breathed in the fresh air and welcomed the positive vibrations of nature surrounding me.

He stepped behind me and pulled me back against him as we gazed out at the impressive sight. It reminded me of when we stood like this at Fair Head, the first time he kissed me. That seems like so long ago, when in fact it wasn't quite two weeks.

It still amazes me that I've only known Conor for such a short time. I feel so connected to him and more comfortable than I did with men I've dated for months or years. In general, I just feel *more*. It should scare the hell out of me, but for some reason it doesn't. Ireland seems to have cast a spell on me and I'm not sure I mind. In fact, it seems to be exactly what I need right now.

"Is that your phone or did you bring a toy for us ta play with?"

He nudged his hips forward and I felt my phone vibrating in my back pocket. I wiggled my butt.

"That's my phone," I said then rested my head on his shoulder and looked back at him. "But I'm open to exploring the toy idea sometime."

"Good ta know," he said with a sexy smirk, then stepped back, took my hand, and led me farther down the path.

We walked to O'Brien's Tower and climbed the narrow spiral staircase all the way to the top. The day is so bright and clear, it seems like we could see forever. And I could have stayed there forever just looking at the view but a large group came, interrupting the peaceful feeling so we left.

After making the trek back to the car, we drove up to County Galway to explore. Our first stop was the Connemara Marble Visitor Centre. I hadn't expected to do much more than check out the museum and visit the shop, but when we arrived a tour of the workshop was starting so we joined.

Our guide showed us the raw materials the crafters work with, which was fascinating. It was also interesting to see jewelry being made then browse the finished products in the shop.

Tears filled my eyes when I spotted a beautiful rosary that Gran would have loved. A sterling silver Celtic cross dangled from hand-crafted marble beads in various shades of green. Before I could talk myself out of it, I picked it up and handed it to the cashier along with my credit card.

"Are ye okay?" Conor asked as we left the store.

I nodded and smiled up at him.

"I will be."

———

AFTER WANDERING around Galway and eating dinner at a local pub, we drove back to the hotel. I'd been nodding off in the car, but got my second wind as soon as Conor mentioned taking a shower.

"Could I maybe talk you into taking a bath in that big tub instead?"

The corner of his mouth kicked up into a sexy smirk.

"It wouldn't take much ta twist my arm, I'll tell ye that."

He walked into the bathroom and I heard the water start running.

"Which do ye prefer?" he asked, holding two bottles out to me.

I took them from him and sniffed. The first smelled like eucalyptus and something else...mint, maybe? It's nice, but not what I wanted. I replaced the cap and opened the second bottle. The aroma of warm vanilla and jasmine filled my senses and I closed my eyes and savored it.

Opening my eyes, I handed the bottle to him.

"This one."

Conor took both bottles from me and disappeared back into the bathroom. When he returned, he brought the rich, musky scent of the bath soap into the bedroom with him. My mouth watered, but I wasn't sure if it was from that or the sight of the man in front of me, bare-chested with his jeans riding low on his hips.

Standing directly in front of me, Conor's eyes held me captive as he ran his index finger across my collarbone, down my chest, between my breasts, and past my belly.

"You won't be needin' this in the bath."

He gripped the hem of my T-shirt with both hands and slowly pulled it up. I lifted my arms and he dragged it over my head and tossed it to the floor. My bra quickly followed.

With his eyes still on mine, he kneeled in front of me and took off my boots one at a time then slipped my socks off my feet. He then popped the button of my jeans and slowly lowered the zipper. I sucked in a breath as he leaned forward and kissed my belly, his warm breath sending goosebumps scattering across my skin.

Sliding his hands back along my waist, he slipped them inside my jeans and cupped my ass, then slowly moved them down, taking my panties along for the ride until they both pooled at my feet.

Conor nibbled at my navel as he slowly crawled forward, which backed me up to the foot of the bed. Pushing me against the edge of the mattress, he shifted closer, his shoulders pushing my legs apart.

My body clenched in anticipation as he dipped his head and trailed open-mouthed kisses up my right thigh. He glanced up at me through impossibly long lashes, his eyes full of promise.

"Watch," his sexy voice commanded.

Oh my.

He leaned forward and gave my pussy an open-mouthed kiss then dipped his tongue inside for a taste. His low groan sent vibrations right through my core and I twisted my fingers into his hair and held on.

Placing his hands on either thigh, he stroked his thumbs over my lips then nudged them apart exposing my clit. I shuddered when he found then teased the tiny nub first with one thumb, then the other. My answering moans increased in volume until they echoed through the room when he replaced his thumbs with his tongue.

He settled into a rhythm designed to make me lose my mind...tease my clit with the tip of his tongue, lap it with the flat, then suck and repeat. Over and over again.

My thighs trembled and he shifted closer, nudging my ass onto the mattress, which tilted my hips forward and opened me up to him even more.

Conor moved his hands down and wrapped them around my ankles then moved my legs up until my calves rested against his shoulders. I grabbed onto the bedspread behind me, trying to keep myself from slipping and just resting on his face. Not that he seemed to mind.

He slid his tongue up and down my slit then slipped one finger inside, then another and pumped in and out adding a whole new sensation. I nearly lost it when he placed his mouth directly over my clit and sucked.

"Oh...Conor...I...ah..."

Apparently my vocabulary had been reduced to single words because I couldn't seem to string a sentence together. Couldn't tell him how good it all felt. Although he seemed to know because he kept on doing it.

I fought to keep my eyes open. Watching him was so hot, so erotic, and I didn't want to miss a single second. But soon both seeing and feeling what he was doing was all too much. His fingers stroking me inside and his tongue teasing me outside brought me higher and higher until I teetered on the edge of a precipice, ready to fall. I panted, trying to hold back, but he was having none of that.

Curling his fingers, he stroked that sweet spot deep inside me then sucked.

"Conor!"

My thighs gripped his head as I shattered into a million pieces.

I rested against the bed and stared at the ceiling as I slowly caught my breath. Conor kissed my hip then shifted up to rest against my body and smiled down at me. His erection poked against my thigh and I was about to move my hand to stroke it when a noise caught my attention. Then I realized what it was.

"Conor!" I screamed for an entirely different reason. "The water!"

Chapter Twenty

CONOR HAD TURNED the taps on low and thankfully he made it to the bathroom to shut the water off before the tub overflowed. We soaked in the warm water and sweet-scented, frothy bubbles until our fingers and toes were both pruney. Then we moved to the shower and it was my turn to get on my knees.

After that I hogged the spray, washing and rinsing my hair while he leaned against the wall and recovered. Once I finished, I left him to shower and slipped into a fluffy hotel robe and curled up in a comfy chair to look out the window at the expansive grounds. I heard a chirping noise and realized it was the voicemail notification on my phone.

Reaching down, I pulled my phone out of my purse, entered my password, and clicked on the app.

THIS MESSAGE IS *for Ruby Devlin. My name is Ed Walley and I'm calling from Coastal Food Distribution. I'm reaching out to discuss an opportunity we have here at CFD. We're expanding into organics and I'd like to talk with you about joining our team to run the division. Full disclosure, we had someone lined up for the position and he decided to go in another direction. So things are moving fast with this. But when I put out feelers, your name was mentioned by several people. The person who gave me your cell number also shared your email so I'll send you some more details to give you a better idea of what's happening here. Please call me back so we can discuss this further. I look forward to hearing from you.*

MY HEART POUNDED as I switched apps and found his email. It's extremely detailed and seemed to imply that the job was mine if I wanted it. Clicking on the attachment, I pulled up the business plan and quickly scrolled through.

The water stopped and I finished reading then dropped my phone into my purse just as Conor walked out of the bathroom. With his slicked-back hair, glistening chest, and towel riding low emphasizing the cut of his hips, the man looked like a walking wet dream.

"Everythin' okay?" he asked.

I nodded, trying to school my features so my feelings didn't show.

"Just enjoying the view."

He smirked and walked toward me.

"I could say the same thing." Resting his hands on the arms of the chair, he leaned down and kissed me. "Are ye hungry? Ye only had soup for dinner." Straightening, he added, "We could order some room service."

"I had that thick Irish seafood chowder with brown bread. Not to mention the Victoria sponge for dessert. So it's not like I didn't eat." I chuckled. "That being said, I wouldn't mind a snack."

He walked over to the desk and found the room service menu then came back over to my side. Taking my hand in his, he pulled me out of the chair just far enough so he could sneak into the seat and pull me onto his lap.

We looked at the menu together and decided to get some appetizers to share instead of full meals. He reached out and grabbed the phone off the end table and called in the order.

"It'll be here in forty-five minutes or so," he said.

"Perfect. By that time, I should be really hungry."

I shifted down and rested my head on his shoulder.

"THIS TRIP HAS BEEN AMAZING, Conor. Thank you."

"Ye don't need ta keep thankin' me. Spending time with ye is a pleasure."

He kissed the top of my head and rubbed his hand up and down my back.

This man is really too good to be true. Every moment we spend together is truly magical and until I got Ed Walley's voicemail, I had no intention of booking a return flight back to Maryland anytime soon. But now that this potential opportunity has fallen in my lap, I'm not sure I have a choice.

"Ye sure yer okay?"

I nodded, not trusting myself to speak. I'm not sure how it happened but Conor Doherty has managed to worm his way into my heart. But I can't abandon everything I've worked for my whole life for a man I've barely known two weeks.

Can I?

Chapter Twenty-One

I STARED at myself in the mirror as I brushed my teeth, trying to figure out what to say to Conor. Wondering if I should even say anything before I have a firm offer in place. But I know that not telling him isn't fair. Besides, he knows something is up.

After rinsing, spitting, and wiping my mouth, I opened the bathroom door and walked into the bedroom. Conor rested in the middle of the bed wearing a pair of loose sweatpants and an old T-shirt. He glanced over at me as I approached and reached his hand out. I took it and he pulled me in for a long, lingering kiss.

He slowly ended the kiss then rested his forehead against mine.

"Are ye gonna tell me what's been botherin' ye or am I gonna have ta keep spinnin' my wheels tryin' ta guess?"

I sat back and looked down at my hands as I twisted my fingers together. There's no way I'll be able to say what I need to if I'm looking into his eyes.

"I got a voicemail last night. It was from a man named

Ed Walley. His company is expanding into organics and he wants to talk to me about running the division."

His hand came into my vision as it rested on top of mine and squeezed. I shifted my gaze to meet his.

"So what happens now?"

"I um—" I cleared my throat. "I have a conference call with him and the other division heads tomorrow night at five o'clock." Turning my hand over, I laced our fingers together. "It's not a done deal."

He pulled our joined hands to his mouth and kissed the back of mine then offered a sad smile. "Oh darlin' of course it is. They'd be crazy ta not want ye."

His image blurred in front of me and I blinked away the tears.

"Come here," he said and held his arms out for me.

I took his invitation and rested my cheek against his chest. His heart raced beneath my ear, letting me know he's not handling my news as calmly as he's letting on.

———

I TOOK a slow walk over to Fiona's. We're having dinner there and Conor headed over earlier so I could have privacy for my phone call. He told me to call and he'd pick me up when I was done, but I figured the walk would give me time to get my thoughts together. But as the house came into view, they were still scattered in a million directions.

Actually, that's a bit of an exaggeration. They're only scattered in two directions...should I stay or should I go?

As I'd thought, the job at Coastal Food Distribution is mine if I want it. It's based in Seattle and comes with a generous salary and bonus plus stock options. Accepting their offer is a no-brainer but I can't ignore the nagging voice in the back of my head telling me to turn it down.

I bypassed the driveway and continued down the road to the path that I know will lead me to the pond. I'm not ready to face everyone yet.

Making my way through the trees, I continued through the high grass and stopped in my tracks as I neared the pond. I must have made a noise, because Conor turned to face me.

I continued forward and he met me in the middle.

"How'd it go?" he asked.

"They offered me the job."

"I told ye they would." He leaned down and kissed my cheek.

My chest ached, as though an elephant was sitting on it, and I struggled to take in air.

This should be one of the happiest days of my life. I didn't have to send out resumes and schmooze my contacts begging for a job. I was offered one based on my reputation in the industry. All my planning and hard work through the years has truly paid off.

If this had happened a month ago, I would have been over the moon with happiness. But looking at the man in front of me, I can't help but wonder what could be if Conor and I were given the chance to spend more time together and let this thing between us grow.

His gray eyes had been glued to mine as all that ran through my head and in true Conor form, he knew exactly what I was thinking. The corner of his mouth curled up into a melancholy smile then he stepped forward, put his arms around me, and held me tight.

"Remember what I said when we met, Ruby. What's meant ta be will be."

Yeah...que será será.

Chapter Twenty-Two

I SAT BACK in my chair and rubbed my eyes. After nearly two weeks of staring at multiple monitors for no less than ten hours a day, they're shot. I could continue what I'm doing but experience has taught me that I'll just end up with a migraine. So I shut down my laptop, undocked it, and loaded it and the files I've been working on into my computer bag then slipped the strap over my shoulder.

Grabbing my raincoat and umbrella, I walked through the empty office and out the front door then took the ramp to the adjacent parking garage. I yawned as I settled into the driver's seat and clicked my seatbelt into place. After looking in my rearview mirror, I backed out of my spot, made my way out of the garage, and headed home. Or what's serving as home at the moment.

I've never been so exhausted in my life. Since leaving Ireland, I've been going non-stop. First I stopped in Maryland just long enough to pack my clothes and close Gran's house. I'm not ready to part with it yet, so for now, I turned its care over to one of her longtime friends, George Baker.

Then I hopped on a plane to Seattle, checked into one of CFD's executive condominiums, and hit the ground running. Besides the fact it will help me get up to speed that much faster, it's also keeping my mind busy so I don't fixate on Conor. As it is, he haunts my dreams. Which is another reason I'm so tired...I'm not sleeping well.

Thankfully traffic was light and I walked through my front door less than ten minutes after pulling out of the parking garage. I dropped my stuff on the kitchen table then walked into the bedroom, changed into old leggings and a T-shirt, and pulled my hair into a ponytail.

I'm not even going to waste time looking in my kitchen for food. I know the cupboards are bare. Instead, I swiped open my phone and ordered Chinese takeout.

The food arrived a half-hour later and I curled into the oversized chair in the living room and flicked on the TV. After flipping through the channels, I settled on *Breaking Bad.* Walter White's situation just might make me feel better about my life. Then again, I'm sure I'm not the only single thirty-four-year-old who's ever eaten Kung Pao Chicken and Pork Fried Rice right out of their containers on a Friday night.

It's funny, I've spent a lot of time alone the past few years, but I never felt lonely until now.

———

THE NEXT TWO weeks were more of the same. Work. Sleep. Repeat. Which is pretty much how I've lived my life for more than a decade, but now it's just not working for me. I used to bask in the glory of a job well done, but for the past month, I've felt unfulfilled. Not to mention unhappy.

Heading this new division is a dream come true, but

I'm starting to realize that maybe it's not *my* dream anymore.

Speaking of dreams. Mine still center on Conor and Ireland but now Gran has started to sneak in too. She keeps handing me something but whenever I look down to see what it is, I wake up. I can't shake the feeling she's trying to tell me something, or at least my subconscious is. Either way, it's driving me crazy that I can't figure it out.

As usual, I left work late on Friday night, but instead of heading to my condo and ordering takeout, I decided to explore the area of Seattle just outside my office building. I walked a few blocks and found myself standing outside an Irish pub. Because I'm a glutton for punishment, I went inside and settled onto a stool at the end of the bar.

The bartender walked over and dropped a coaster in front of me.

"What can I get ye?"

Oh dear Lord, he has an Irish accent.

I blinked away tears.

"I'll have a pint of Guinness and a glass of water," I said. "And can I also see a menu?"

He handed me the menu then walked over to the tap to pour my drink. When he placed it in front of me, I asked for an order of fish and chips.

I took a long drink, thinking how much better Guinness tasted in Ireland. I have no idea if it actually is different there or if it's the people and atmosphere that makes it seem that way.

The bartender stepped up to a microphone across the room and introduced the band. I almost choked on my next drink when the first notes of *Livin' on a Prayer* sounded through the speakers.

I longed to call Conor and share the moment, but I know I can't do that. After spending our last two days in

Ireland together, he made slow, sweet love to me one last time, then drove me to the airport and dropped me off. We both agreed that he shouldn't accompany me to the gate. We also agreed that we shouldn't stay in touch. It would be too painful.

The bartender was back, and this time he placed a large platter of fish and chips in front of me. He reached under the bar and pulled out a bottle of malt vinegar, silverware, and extra napkins. After I assured him I didn't need anything else, he walked away to check on the people at the other end of the bar.

I set the small cup of coleslaw on the side of the plate then sprinkled vinegar over the fish filet and mound of chips. My mouth watered in anticipation of my first bite.

The band switched to *I'm Shipping Up To Boston* by Dropkick Murphys. That also made me itch to call Conor because I hadn't included them in my list of pub-appropriate bands in our discussion at Brady's.

I cleared my plate and emptied my pint but instead of going home, decided to stay and listen to the band a little while longer. They're playing a fun mix of rock and Irish rock and by the time they ended their first set, I felt more relaxed than I have in a month.

As tempted as I was to stay, have another pint, and listen to the next set, I decided to head out. I have a feeling that if I go home now and get into bed, I'll be able to get a good night's sleep.

Chapter Twenty-Three

I WOKE SLOWLY, drifting in that space between sleep and full consciousness for several minutes before opening my eyes. Rolling onto my back, I stared at the ceiling, a huge smile on my face. Not only did I get a good night's sleep, but I finished my dream. I finally know what Gran was trying to tell me.

Like usual, I'd dreamed of Conor, but instead of reliving the angst of our parting, my head filled with snapshots of his smiling face. Then his image faded away and I was leaving Gran's house and she followed me onto the porch and handed me something. I looked down and saw it was a crochet square of the Doherty crest.

She was smiling when I glanced back up at her and I heard her beautiful, lilting voice in my head.

"Go. Be happy."

Then she disappeared and I was here in my bed.

I don't need a psychologist to analyze that dream for me.

And I don't care if it's just my own psyche leading me

back to Ireland, I can't deny anymore that it's where I belong.

———

ED WALLEY WAS SHOCKED when I handed him my resignation on Monday, but I'm happy to say, he didn't take me up on my offer to give notice. I used the old breakup line and assured him it wasn't the company, it was me.

It took HR a day to put my final paperwork together so I had to come in today to sign that and hand in my laptop and cell phone. Per protocol, security accompanied me to my office where there was an empty box sitting in the center of my desk. Other than my framed picture of Gran that I was able to drop into my purse, I haven't personalized the space at all. So I have nothing else to take with me.

I took one last look around the corner office and smiled. Walking away from the thing I worked so hard to achieve should be bittersweet, but it's just sweet. After all, I'm moving on to a life that will suit who I am now. As I exited the building, I didn't feel sad or scared or regretful. I just feel free.

I'd packed up all my business attire over the weekend and so after leaving the office, I headed straight to Dress for Success and dropped it off. Then I stopped at the car dealership to turn in my leased vehicle. After signing the paperwork and handing in my fobs, I picked up my suitcase, left the building, and called an Uber to take me to the airport.

Chapter Twenty-Four

IRELAND GREETED ME WITH RAIN, but that's not going to dampen my spirits. After making my way through customs, I headed toward the restroom to freshen up. Considering the fact I've been traveling for nearly twenty-four hours, I don't look too awful. I splashed cold water on my face, moisturized, then applied basic makeup, brushed my hair, and called it good.

I left the ladies' room and headed toward ground transportation to find a taxi. There was a long line, but within ten minutes, I was in the back seat of a Toyota Prius, heading toward Ballyclare.

I'm equal parts excited and anxious about seeing Conor. We didn't exactly end on bad terms but we did end because I chose my career over him. Still, I'm here with the hope he still wants me in his life.

I have no idea what I'm going to say when I see him again. Other than figuring out how to get him in my presence, I haven't planned a thing. I'm getting kind of addicted to this go-with-the-flow thing.

My view of the landscape was obstructed when the

light shower turned into a full-blown downpour. Just like the last time I made this journey. Hopefully it's a good sign.

The ride from Belfast takes less than a half-hour, but seemed like an eternity. When the driver turned off the main road, I picked up my phone and switched it to selfie mode to check my face. Although, with the way it's raining, I'll probably look like a drowned rat just like I did last time I arrived in Ballyclare. I mentally shrugged. At least I won't be caked with mud.

The driver turned into the parking lot and pulled as close to the door as possible. After paying him and giving a generous tip, I grabbed my bag and was pelted by rain as I got out. Splashing through the puddles, I walked the few feet from the car to the door and yanked it open.

Four familiar sets of eyes turned to face me and I smiled.

"Hello Jack. Shane. Marty. Jamie." I nodded at each of the men in turn.

With the way things are here, I'm sure they all know that Conor and I were involved. They also know I left. Hopefully that won't keep them from helping me out.

"Don' tell me ye crashed again," Jamie said.

"No, not this time." I settled onto the same stool I sat on last time I was here. "But I'm going to ask you to call for a tow truck." He raised his right brow and I added, "And can you make sure Conor is the one who comes?"

A smile spread across his face as he caught on. Turning around, he reached for the phone and dialed.

"Conor, it's Jamie Kelly. We need the tow truck over here." He nodded, then looked over and gave a thumb's up. "I'll tell them," he said and hung up.

Grabbing the bottle of Bushmills, he walked over to me then reached under the bar, grabbed a glass, and set it in front of me

"He'll be here shortly," he said as he poured. "He's helpin' Ronan with somethin'."

I'm not sure I should be drinking on so little sleep, but I'll take my chances. I took a sip, welcoming the warmth it spread through me. In a few short minutes, I'll see Conor again. Before I could overthink that too much, Jamie spoke.

"So, yer here fer good?"

I nodded. "I'm here for good."

Seemingly satisfied with my answer, the four men took turns filling me in on what I missed while I was gone. I leaned my elbow against the bar, hanging on their every word.

I'd just finished my whiskey when I heard the door open behind me.

"Who needs the tow, Jamie?"

Jamie nodded in my direction and I felt Conor walk up behind me.

I closed my eyes and took in a shaky breath before turning around to face him. He looks just as spectacular as he did the first time I saw him. Only instead of saying something stupid like "oh wow" I couldn't speak at all.

"So ye need a tow?" I shook my head and he frowned "Ye don't need a tow?" Again I shook my head. "So what do ye need?"

I know he saw the answer to that question in my eyes, but I can see that he needs to hear the words.

"You." My voice cracked and I cleared my throat. "I need you."

I barely got the words out when he leaned down and brushed his lips gently against mine. He nudged my thighs apart and stepped closer. I followed his lead when he opened his mouth and brushed his tongue against mine.

Oh how I've missed this. The feel of him. The taste of him. It's just so damn good.

How could a man I've only known for a couple weeks become as essential to me as the air I breathe?

I don't know the answer to that question but I do know it's true. He's what was missing from my life when I left. But now that we're together, I feel whole again.

The sound of a bar stool scraping against the floor reminded us that we're not alone and he slowly ended the kiss. Reaching down, he picked up my suitcase with one hand then held out the other for me to take.

"Thanks Jamie," he said as he led me out the door to his truck.

I climbed inside and he closed the door behind me. The back door opened and he tossed my suitcase inside before opening the driver's side door and settling behind the steering wheel.

I thought he'd kiss me again once we were alone, but instead, he started the truck, shifted into drive, and drove out of the parking lot. A few minutes later, we were pulling into his garage. Without saying a word, we got out and walked up to his apartment. He set my suitcase on the floor and stalked over to me.

Placing his hands on either side of my face, he leaned down and placed a sweet kiss on my mouth, then pulled back.

"Ruby, I didn't tell ye before, but I love ye," he said. "I love ye so much, I'm hurtin' with it."

"I love you too."

"Ya?"

"Yeah." My heart melted at his sweet smile and I finally found my voice. "I don't quit my job, get rid of all my corporate clothes, and move to a different country for just anyone."

His eyes widened with every word.

"Yer really here fer good?"

"I'm really here for good."

"Oh thank God."

He crushed his mouth to mine again and we both poured our every emotion into the kiss. It was loving and desperate and needy. Pulling back, Conor bent down, picked me up, and carried me to the bedroom.

There was no finesse. As soon as he set me down, we both ripped our clothes off and met in the center of the bed. We were both desperate for each other's touch and our hands and mouths roamed, our movements frantic.

I rested back against the pillows and let out a long low groan when Conor moved between my thighs and plunged inside. Wrapping my arms and legs around him, I held on as he pumped in and out, every deep thrust taking me higher and higher.

"Conor...oh God...don't stop..."

"Ruby," he panted. "I can't hold on...it feels too good...missed ye so much..."

"Missed you too...love you..."

He gripped my hips and tilted them up and his pelvis brushed against my clit with every forward thrust. That's all it took to shove me over the edge and I dragged him along with me.

After we caught our breath, Conor shifted onto his side and pulled me against his chest.

"I'm so happy yer back. I missed ye every second of every day."

I wrapped my arm around his waist and squeezed.

"It was the same for me."

"Still, I can't believe ye gave up yer whole life ta come back."

I shifted back to look at him.

"Conor, my life was empty without you. So I've gained more coming here than I left behind." I smiled. "But just so you know, I don't have a place to stay," I said.

"So even after what happened last time ye were here, ye hopped on a plane with no plan again?"

"A wise man once told me that what's meant to be will be."

"A wise man, huh?"

"Very wise," I said. "He also told me that if I trust my instincts, I'll end up where I'm meant to be. When I left, every fiber of my being was screaming at me that it was a mistake. I should've listened. It would have saved us both a lot of heartache."

He tucked my hair behind my ear and smiled.

"Well yer here now and that's all that matters."

Epilogue

Four months later

CONOR and I sat next to each other holding hands, the lights of the waiting room glistening off the gorgeous cushion-cut diamond he'd given me. I looked down and smiled. The sight of the platinum band circling the third finger on his left hand is still one of my favorite things.

He proposed the day after I returned and we married a month later. I was never one of those girls who grew up dreaming about my wedding so when planning the big day, I let Fiona run with it. And she'd enjoyed every single second, not to mention did a great job.

We got married at the church then returned to the house for a reception that lasted until dawn. The entire day was perfect...the weather, the food, the guests, and most especially the groom.

Both the Doherty and Brady families have welcomed me with open arms and I'm enjoying being part of such a large clan. Ronan, Brady, and Mac all gave speeches at the wedding that were a perfect combination of teasing and heartfelt. They've adopted me as the sister they never had and I'm enjoying the role.

And Fiona and Paddy have been amazing. They've embraced me as their daughter...no *in-law* allowed.

I'd told Fiona about the dream that persuaded me to come back and she's convinced it really was Gran reaching out. Then she made me cry like a baby on our wedding day when she presented Conor and me with a throw she'd knitted with the Doherty crest in the center.

"Ye nervous?"

"No, just anxious," I said. "I'll be relieved when this is done so I can hang around your mom again. It's been tough staying away but I knew if I saw her, I'd crack."

"Mac said she yelled at him for workin' ye too hard."

"That's kind of my fault," I said with a chuckle. "I told her he booked a bunch of projects with short deadlines."

Working with Mac has been amazing. It's challenging, fulfilling, and fun. And best of all, my schedule is flexible so I can spend a lot of time with my new husband.

"Ruby Doherty."

My new name still makes me smile.

"That's me," I said as Conor and I both stood and followed the woman into the room she'd emerged from.

She closed the door behind us.

"My name is Maggie. Ye can hop up on the bed," she said to me, then added to Conor. "If ye sit in that chair ye'll be able ta see everythin'."

I relaxed onto the bed and she had me lift my shirt and pull my pants down enough to expose my stomach.

"This might be a little cold," she said and squirted gel...which *was* cold...onto my slightly-rounded belly.

The night Conor and I were reunited, we were too

caught up in the moment to use a condom and since I didn't have a need for it, I stopped taking birth control two years ago. It's funny neither one of us panicked when we realized we'd had unprotected sex. I'm getting pretty good with this what-will-be-will-be lifestyle.

And what happened was a baby.

Without the pill, my cycles were pretty irregular so by the time I realized I was pregnant, I was almost four months along.

As she pressed the transducer to my stomach, black and white images filled the screen. Conor leaned his elbow onto the bed next to my hip, his hand gripping mine.

She passed it over my skin, going back and forth a couple times before stopping.

"Ah, that's what we're lookin' fer. There's your baby."

The image on the screen blurred and I blinked away tears then smiled back at Conor and found him doing the same. He returned my smile and kissed the back of my hand.

"There's the heartbeat. And there's the head and the spine."

A white arrow moved across the image as she continued to narrate what we were seeing. Once she pointed out the head, it was easier to make things out. She took measurements as she went along, assuring us that everything looked great.

"Do ye want ta know the sex?"

"Yes, please," Conor and I said in unison.

She moved the transducer, then changed the view on the screen, and frowned.

"I'm gonna have ye move onto yer side."

"Is everything okay?" I asked as I rolled.

Instead of answering, she continued to move the transducer and study the monitor.

I looked over my shoulder at Conor and even though he gave my hand a reassuring squeeze, he looked as worried as I felt.

"Well lookee that," Maggie said with a smile. "Ye were hidin'."

"What?" I cringed at my shrill tone.

She froze the image on the screen and used her index finger to circle two areas.

"Congratulations, yer havin' twin girls."

"Did ye say twins?" Conor asked. She nodded and he looked at me, a smile spreading across his face. "Twins," he repeated.

"Twin girls," I said.

Maggie hit a few buttons on the keyboard and pictures started coming out of the printer on the counter. She picked up a box of tissues and placed it on the table next to me.

"Ye can get cleaned up." She stood. "I'll give ye a few minutes."

She left the room, closing the door behind her.

I rolled onto my back and smiled up at Conor. He reached over and pulled a handful of tissues from the box and used them to wipe the gel from my stomach then he leaned down and placed a kiss right in the center.

"This is amazin'. I didn't think I could get any happier, then this happens. We're truly blessed," he said.

A quick knock sounded on the door and Maggie came back inside. She pulled the pictures from the printer and handed them to me. Conor and I stared at them, still in awe.

"A video of the ultrasound and all the measurements will be sent ta yer doctor," she said. "I'm sure I'll be seein' ye again. She usually does these regularly with multiples."

I sat and Conor held my hand as I slipped my way off the bed.

"Thank you so much," I said as we followed her back out to the waiting room.

Conor pressed the button and the elevator doors immediately opened. We stepped inside and he wrapped his arms around me and held me tight.

"Where should we go celebrate our good news?"

I shifted back just enough to look into his eyes

"Is that a serious question?" I asked. "We need to go tell your mom. She needs to know that she has to get bunk beds for the pink room."

His laugh echoed through the elevator just before we reached the ground floor and the doors opened.

"Come on." He stepped back and laced his fingers through mine. "Let's go spread the good news."

The End

Loving London

Loving

LONDON

Chapter One

LONDON

"I CAN'T BELIEVE it's been a year." I blinked until my aunt's face wasn't blurry anymore. "Some days it seems like she's been gone forever and others I expect her to be home when I walk through the door."

"Yeah, I still pick up my phone to call or text her at least three times a day."

Aunt Maisie and I are sitting in my mom's favorite ice cream parlor to observe the first anniversary of her death. Being here is bittersweet. I have so many great memories here with my mom, but the fact that we won't make any more is beyond painful.

I looked down at my half-eaten sundae. Brownie a la mode made with mint chocolate chip ice cream was my mother's most recent favorite. We came here often enough that she experimented with most things on the menu. That was especially true when she started chemo and her taste changed.

"You know, I thought that when a whole year had passed, it would be easier." Glancing over at Aunt Maisie, I shook my head. "But it's not. I still cry just about every day, and that underlying feeling of sadness is still there."

She set her spoon down and reached out to squeeze my hand.

"Grief is fluid. You'll have good days and bad, but unfortunately, it's never going to totally go away," she said. "But it'll get easier, I promise."

"I'm sorry." I pulled my hand out from under hers and wiped the tears off my cheeks. "Sometimes I forget that you've already been through this with your father and my dad."

"It's not surprising you don't remember them. You were so young when they died."

My dad was one of the hundreds of firefighters who died during the 9/11 attacks. My grandfather had a fatal heart attack a couple weeks after his funeral. I was only three years old. Growing up, I felt their absence, but didn't experience grief like this.

Shaking my head, I picked up my spoon and filled it with equal amounts of brownie and ice cream.

"But we're here to honor mom's memory, so let's keep things upbeat."

I held up my full spoon as if to toast and shoved the bite into my mouth, taking some comfort in the sweet minty flavor. We were both silent as we finished our ice cream. A few minutes later, she pushed her bowl away and rested her forearms against the edge of the table.

"There's something I want to talk to you about."

My stomach tightened at the look on her face. What's making me nervous is the fact that she's trying to act chill, but her eyes are telling me she's anything but.

"Okay."

"Don't look so worried. It's not bad, I promise."

"Well, you look nervous about something."

She took a sip of water then set the glass down and focused on her fingers wrapped around its base as she spoke.

"There's something your mom and I talked about before she passed away." Her gaze shifted up to meet mine. "She wanted me to make sure you go to England like you two had planned."

"We planned on taking that trip together." I shook my head. "It wouldn't be the same without her."

After high school, my mom spent a gap year in England, and according to her, it changed her life. Tales of her travels were my bedtime stories and I dreamed about the day I'd experience them for myself. Through the years, we planned our own trip and saved pennies to make it happen. We were supposed to go the summer after I graduated high school, but that spring she was diagnosed with colon cancer. Aside from the fact she didn't feel physically capable of traveling, the money we'd saved went to pay for her treatments.

"London, you're stuck." I opened my mouth to speak, but she continued. "You've been through a lot, so it's understandable, but it's time to start moving forward. Your mom thought getting away and experiencing a new place might help shake things up for you."

"The thing is, I'm not really a *shaking things up* kind of girl. That was more my mom."

"Your mom was pretty fearless, but you have that in you, too."

"I'm not sure about that. There's no way I'd take off to England by myself after high school like she did." I snorted. "I'm twenty-five, and can't imagine doing it."

"Don't underestimate yourself. You were there for your

mom and took care of her through her entire illness. That takes a lot of courage."

I didn't know how to respond to that so I focused on the melted remains in my bowl.

"Besides," Aunt Maisie said. "You won't be alone."

I nearly gave myself whiplash jerking my head up to look at her.

"You're coming with me?"

"No."

"Why not? It'll be so fun."

"It'd be a blast, but I couldn't leave Jackie and Ava that long."

I nodded in understanding, then her last two words sunk in.

"How long?"

"Your mom had hoped for six months, which is the max you're able to stay there without a visa, but I talked her down to three."

"Three months?" My voice echoed off the walls. I looked around, offering an apologetic smile to the other patrons. "I can't go away for three months," I said in a lower tone.

"Why not?"

"For one, I have work."

"That's another part of this."

"Whatis?"

"Lo, it's time to quit your job."

"I can't quit my job."

"The job at the coffee shop wasn't supposed to be permanent."

"It's not."

"You graduated college three years ago. Why are you still working there?"

A bunch of reasons were on the tip of my tongue, but I

knew Aunt Maisie would recognize them for what they are…excuses. The truth is, I'm still working there because it's easy and comfortable.

"Mom's life insurance gave me a little bit of a financial cushion, but I can't afford to go to England for three months. Especially if I don't have a job to come home to."

"Your mom had a pension from an old job that offered a buyout a couple years ago. She took the money and invested it, naming me beneficiary. If her cancer went into remission, she figured you two would use it to take your trip. Otherwise, she wanted me to plan this trip for you."

Resting my elbows on the table, I rubbed my temples. This is a lot to process. There are worse things in the world than being told you're going on an extended trip to England, but my head is still spinning.

"You said I wouldn't be alone."

I raised my voice on the last word, turning my sentence into a question.

"Oh right," she said. "Remember your mom's friend Sharon?"

"Yes."

The two had met when my mom was on her British adventure and stayed in touch through the years. She and her son even visited about fifteen years ago when they were over here visiting family.

"Her husband Sebastian is a college professor and also gives tours. They're going to show you around," she said. "Sharon knows the places your mom wanted to take you and she's really excited to see you again."

Tears filled my eyes at the thought of taking this trip without my mom, but it's something she wanted me to do.

"It won't be the same without her," I whispered.

"I know, but the change of scenery will be good for you. The last few years have been so stressful. Go and enjoy yourself." She reached over and squeezed my hand. "Sharon will take good care of you."

I nodded and looked around at the old-fashioned decor, processing everything Aunt Maisie said. Going on this trip without my mom will be bittersweet, like coming to this ice cream parlor. But that's not stopping me from coming here, so it shouldn't prevent me from taking the trip.

"When do I leave?"

"Three weeks."

I nodded, then took a deep breath in through my nose and blew it out my mouth.

"That doesn't give me much time."

"For what?"

"To figure out how to pack for three months without bringing a steamer trunk."

BAS

MY MOUTH WATERED AS I stepped through the back door of my parents' house.

"Something smells good."

"I've made jammy dodgers."

My mum pointed toward the platter on the kitchen table.

"What's the occasion?" I sat and reached for a jam-filled biscuit and ate half in one bite. "Mmm, blackberry is my favorite."

"I know." She settled into the chair across from me. "That's why I made them."

Stuffing the remaining half of the biscuit into my

mouth, I scrutinized her as I chewed and swallowed. When she texted and asked me to "pop over" when I could spare a bit, I figured she needed me to get something off a top shelf or pick up a heavy box. But between the jammy dodgers and the cheeky grin on her face, I'm guessing there's something else happening here.

"Just say it."

"What?"

I raised my brow and reached for another biscuit. Strawberry this time.

"It's quite clear you've got something on your mind."

She leaned her forearms against the edge of the table and folded her hands together.

"You remember Jane, my pal from the States?" I nodded. "She'd been meaning to bring her daughter London here for an extended break, but with the whole cancer situation, that never came to pass. Now that Jane's no longer with us, London's planning a solo trip for three months. I've assured her aunt that we'll keep an eye out and give her the grand tour."

I relaxed at that. My father acts as a tour guide occasionally. Being a history professor, his head is brimming with all sorts of titbits that really jazz up his tours.

"It's really a shame that Jane never got around to bringing her over, but I'm certain you and dad will make sure she has a grand time," I said. "Will she be staying here?" Then I realized what this conversation must be about. "Do you want me to clear out of the carriage house? I could stay at my cottage. It's a wreck, but I'll make do."

"There's no need for you to move out, she'll be staying in the guest room. But I was thinking it'd be quite nice if you were to be her guide, rather than your dad and me."

"Why me?"

"The poor dear has had a rough go of it and could do with a break. I think she'll have more fun with you than your stodgy parents," she said with a nervous chuckle. "And the timing is spot on, what with you having completed that major project and planning to take a break."

"Ma, I'm taking a break to work on the cottage."

"I didn't mean to imply that you need to be in the girl's company every moment of the day. You'll manage to fit your work in."

"You know all the work I have planned. They're not projects I can do in fits and starts, and I've already torn some things apart in anticipation of having time to put them back together."

"I know you're keen on getting the cottage finished, but it's not like you don't have a place to live. Your father and I certainly aren't pushing you to leave here."

Whilst my father is what my grandfather charmingly labels a "poor academic," mum's side of the family is firmly entrenched in the upper crust, and we've always enjoyed the privileges that come with that. This house was given to my parents as a wedding present. It's spacious enough that if my sister and I decided not to leave, even as adults, we'd still have plenty of room. However, during the lockdown, I took over the carriage house, and Elsie headed to London last year. Still, at the age of twenty-seven, it's high time I should be living on my own, particularly given that I have my own place. A place, I might add, also gifted to me by my grandparents.

"The cottage has been mine for two years now and I haven't done more than tidy the yard and demo the upstairs. If I don't knuckle down and get on with it, I'll never get it done."

"That's a touch dramatic, don't you think?"

"No."

"London isn't the only one who needs a bit of fun," she said. "You've been working non-stop. I thought freelance work would be more flexible."

So did I, but my inbox has been flooded with opportunities. I didn't plan to get on the hamster wheel, doing one project after another, but somehow it happened. It's been a boost for my bank account, but hell on my social life.

"I have a list of repairs and renovations that need my attention," I said, making a last effort to avoid giving in.

"Sebastian, you're too young to act so old," she said.

I cringed at her use of my proper name.

"I don't act old."

"When did you last have a proper outing with your mates?" I sighed, resisting the urge to roll my eyes, mostly because I don't remember. "The house can wait. A bit of fresh air and socializing will do you a world of good. London is only here for three months. If there's something you desperately need to do, dad and I will take over for the day. Otherwise, I expect you'll show her around."

I sighed again, running a hand through my hair. I grudgingly have to acknowledge her point. It's been weeks since I've spent time with anyone other than her and Dad. But still…

Mum watched me with a cat-that-ate-the-cream look on her face. She's well aware that regardless of how much I object, I'll end up doing exactly as she asks.

I took a deep breath in through my nose and blew it out my mouth.

"Fine, I'll do it," I said. "When is she coming?"

"Next Friday." She tucked a strand of hair behind her ear and smiled. "I'll send you her flight details and the list of places her mum wanted her to visit. You and London plan the schedule as you see fit."

"I'm picking her up from the airport, too?"

"Of course. That'll give you time to get acquainted on the ride home," she said. "Or rather, re-acquainted as you've already met."

Visions of a pudgy girl with strawberry-blonde hair and bright green eyes popped into my head. She'd been quiet and was more content with her nose in a book than socializing. Hopefully that's changed or it's going to be a long three months.

Chapter Two

LONDON

"I'M IMPRESSED."

"Why?"

Aunt Maisie pointed at the suitcase and backpack sitting in the foyer.

"That's all you have?" I nodded. "For three months?"

"Sharon reminded me that I'll be able to wash clothes, so I didn't need to bring a ton. Still, the suitcase barely zipped and all my toiletries are in the backpack." I checked my purse for the hundredth time, making sure my passport and pounds were in there. "I brought one of those fold-up bags in case I need extra space coming home."

"I'm sure you'll find a lot of good souvenirs," she said. "Promise me you'll treat yourself."

"This whole trip is a treat, especially since you upgraded me to first class."

"You deserve it." She gave me a quick side hug. "Come on. We better get going just in case we hit traffic."

After a just-in-case trip to the bathroom, we were on the road, heading for BWI. As we drove, I mentally checked through the list of what I packed, trying to figure out if I forgot anything. I think I'm good, but since we're halfway to the airport, it's not like we're turning around. My passport, cash, and credit cards are the only things I absolutely need. Anything else can be purchased.

Maisie glanced over at me and smiled, "Are you getting excited?"

"Yeah."

She chuckled.

"Could you make that sound more convincing?"

"I am excited," I said. "But three months is a long time."

"You'll be in good hands." She patted my knee. "I expect you to send me lots of pictures of your adventures."

"Oh, that reminds me. Don't forget, if you want to talk to me, call through WhatsApp. Or you can Facetime or video through Facebook messenger. My cell plan doesn't include international calls, just texts."

"Got it," she said. "I'll probably text everyday like usual, but I'll wait for you to call. I don't want to interrupt your fun."

"You could never interrupt my fun. You're the fun aunt, remember?"

"How could I forget? I'm the one who brainwashed you into thinking that."

Our laughter filled the car and we talked about adventures we've had together through the years. Before long, Maisie turned off the airport exit and pulled over in the drop-off section. We got out of the car and I grabbed my suitcase and backpack from the trunk.

Even though I've had three weeks to mentally prepare for this, I wasn't surprised when my eyes filled with tears. But I was surprised to see tears in Aunt Maisie's eyes.

"Have the time of your life." She pulled me into a hug and held me tight. "I'm so happy you're going, but I'm going to miss you like hell."

Loosening her hold, she kissed my forehead before stepping back.

"I'm going to miss you, too." I pulled the handle up on my suitcase and slipped my backpack over it. "I'll let you know when I land."

"Let me know when you take off, too."

"Will do."

And after another long hug, I grabbed the handle of the suitcase and rolled it behind me as I walked through the automatic doors and into the airport. I took a deep breath and looked around, then followed the signs to security. Thankfully the line wasn't too long and I was heading to my gate in no time.

I settled into a seat and looked around. It's still a bit surreal that I'm doing this. I'll be getting on a plane shortly and won't be back for three months. And when I get home, I'll have to find a job.

Shaking those last thoughts out of my head, I pulled my AirPods out of my purse and popped them into my ears. Scrolling through my phone, I turned on my favorite true crime podcast and sat back to people watch.

Listening to soothing music might be a better choice before I take my first solo flight but for some reason, I find the podcasts relaxing. I usually go to sleep with the sounds of murder and mayhem in my ears.

I'm determined to enjoy this trip, and the fact that Aunt Maisie purchased a first class seat should help with the flight portion. I still can't believe she did that. But based on the number of people in the gate area, I'm guessing the plane is full, so I'm extra grateful for the upgrade.

My podcast episode finished and I noticed that people were starting to stand and collect their luggage. I took out my AirPods just as the announcement was made that boarding was going to begin. Since I'm in the first group, I was on the plane and settled into my little suite in no time.

I don't like going into anything blind, so I'd Googled exactly what my seat was going to look like. After watching at least ten YouTube videos showing the layout, I'm still amazed at how much space I have. From what I saw, the seat fully reclines, which will be nice. Since I'm flying through the night and landing in the morning, I'm hoping to get some sleep. I'd hate to be a total zombie when I see Sharon again for the first time in more than a decade.

The flight attendant walked over, offering a glass of champagne. I was going to ask for water instead, but then reached for the glass. Might as well start my adventure right from the start.

After removing my shoes and sliding on the slippers the airline provided, I grabbed my iPad and settled into my seat. I know there are shows and movies to stream on the plane, but I downloaded a British moviefest to watch. So now I have to decide between *Notting Hill*, *What a Girl Wants*, the *Bridget Jones* trilogy, and *Love Actually*. I probably won't make it through more than two movies if I want to take a nap, but it's good to have choices.

The captain gave the announcement to lock the door and prepare for takeoff. The flight attendant came by to collect my now-empty glass and shortly after, we started to move. My stomach tightened as we taxied down the runway. In order to distract myself from the takeoff itself, I grabbed my iPad and popped in my AirPods. After scrolling through my downloads, I decided on *What a Girl Wants*. Daphne Reynolds was only seventeen when she took off for London in search of her father. Things worked out well for her. Even though it's just a movie, it gives me hope they'll work out for me, too.

———

BAS

I STOOD IN THE TERMINAL, utterly flabbergasted that Mum somehow persuaded me not only to fetch London Spencer from the airport but also to be her personal tour guide for the next three months. I'm thinking that once she's comfortable being in a new place, she'll want to explore on her own. So I'll probably be off duty after a few weeks.

The door to the gate opened and people walked past me to get closer. I'm tall enough to see over the crowd, so I stayed back. I know what London looks like, or at least think I do. It's been over a decade since I've seen her last, but remember her unique shade of strawberry blonde hair. Just in case, as passengers began to emerge, I held up the sign mum had made with London Spencer written in bold, black letters.

With people constantly knocking into me as they exited the gate area, I decided to move to the side and lean against a pillar. I hadn't spotted anyone familiar and passengers were still emerging, so I was surprised when someone tapped me on the shoulder. I looked down at the woman next to me.

"I'm London Spencer."

My eyes widened. It was on the tip of my tongue to ask

if she was sure, but remembered my manners at the last minute.

"I'm Bas," I said, then added, "Middleton."

She held out her hand and I couldn't look away as I shook it. Her once bright hair had darkened to a warm coppery brown, which makes her green eyes even more striking. Realizing I was holding her hand longer than is socially acceptable, I released it and took a small step back, putting my hands in my pockets.

"You cut your hair," she said.

"Pardon?"

"Last time I saw you, your hair was almost at your shoulders."

Funny she's noticing my hair, too.

"Ah yes, the long-hair phase my mum hated," I said. "That only lasted a year. Sad that's how you had to see it."

She chuckled and looked around.

"Is your mom here?"

"No, she sent me to collect you." I looked at the small roller bag and backpack next to her. "How many more bags do you have?"

"This is it."

"Really?" She nodded. "That's…shocking."

Taking hold of the handle, I started walking toward the exit, with London following along.

"Why is it shocking?"

"My sister would bring more than this to go away for a weekend. I'm actually impressed." I pointed to another sign. "Do you need to use the loo?"

She shifted her gaze between me and the sign.

"How long is the ride?"

"If there's no traffic, it's about an hour and fifteen."

"Then yes."

I waited off to the side as she went into the ladies,

trying to wrap my mind around my initial reaction to her. As Mum pointed out, my social life has been non-existent the past few years, and that includes dating. My last proper girlfriend was nearly two years back, and since then, I've been too tied up to really search for someone new. There've been occasional flings, but no one that's really stood out. That *lack* must explain my twisting gut and pounding heart when I first laid eyes on London. Before I had to dig too deep, she returned.

"Ready?"

"Yep."

London and I made polite conversation as we walked to the car. Her flight was good. She managed to sleep a little, thanks to her first class seat. The weather is beautiful today and is expected to be for the next few days.

"I wasn't sure how much luggage you'd have, so I brought Mum's car," I said as we approached the Volvo. Opening the boot, I set her bags inside and slammed it closed. "But this would have fit in my car."

"This is actually the first type of car I've recognized. All the others are different from what's back home."

She walked to the driver's side. I stepped around to the other side and chuckled as I opened the door.

"If you don't mind, I'd like to drive."

Her brow furrowed, then she realized her error. She walked around the front of the car and her clean scent filled my nostrils as she stepped around me and settled into the passenger seat.

"Sorry about that."

"No worries."

I sat behind the wheel and pulled out of the car park. London looked out her window as I merged onto the M40. I drove along, feeling at ease with the silence between us. Which is odd, because we're basically strangers.

The clean scent I noticed earlier is now filling the car. It's a blend of citrus and something else. Perhaps vanilla? I inhaled deeply, letting the fragrance tease my senses. I was so lost trying to figure it out, I startled when she spoke.

"It's funny. If I wasn't sitting on this side of the car and not driving, I could convince myself we're in Maryland. The scenery is so similar." She looked over at me. "I wonder if the other places your mom plans on taking me will be similar."

"Some are and some aren't," I said, then figured I should let her in on the new plan. "And actually, Mum has asked if I'd show you around."

"Oh."

It's unclear if that's a happy sound or not, but I continued explaining.

"She thought you'd have more fun with me than my 'stodgy parents.'" I used air quotes on those last two words. "She'll be around if I'm busy and to do girly things, like afternoon tea, but otherwise you're stuck with me. If that's okay," I added, realizing I'm blindsiding her with this information.

Her mouth curled into a small smile and she nodded.

"Yeah, it's okay."

"Brilliant."

As we continued on in silence, I couldn't help but think that maybe the next three months won't be so bad after all.

Chapter Three

LONDON

BAS TURNED into the driveway and my eyes widened at
the sight in front of me.

"This is your house?"

I cringed at my screechy tone.

We drove past the front of the enormous stone structure and continued around the back. I spotted an old stone
wall in the far distance of a perfectly manicured, impossibly green lawn. A variety of trees dotted the property and
hedges along the side making it feel like we're in the middle
of nowhere, when I know for a fact there are houses on
either side.

"It's my parents' house," he said. "I'm actually living in
their carriage house until I renovate my cottage."

I expected him to continue to the garage at the end of
the driveway, but instead, he stopped next to the back door,
which flew open as we stepped out of the car.

Sharon scurried across the patio and placed her hands on my shoulders.

"Look at you. You're so lovely."

She pulled me into a hug and squeezed me tight. When I realized my arms were just awkwardly hanging at my sides, I raised my hands as far as her embrace would allow and rested them against either side of her waist. We stood like that forever until she finally released me.

"How was your flight?" she asked as she shifted and placed her arm around my shoulders, then led me inside.

"It was good," I said as I looked around the kitchen then back at her. "Thank you so much for having me here. Your home is beautiful."

Granted, I've only seen the outside and now the kitchen, but it stands to reason, the rest is just as spectacular.

"No thanks necessary. I'm chuffed you're here."

I must have looked confused because Bas chuckled as he set my bags down.

"That means she's pleased," he said.

"Oh." I shifted my gaze in Sharon's direction and she nodded. "Good."

"I made a light lunch," she said. "Bas will show you to your room while I set the table."

Bas picked up my bags again and gestured for me to precede him out of the kitchen. I froze as I entered the formal dining room.

"Wow."

The space is both elegant and inviting, with a huge stone fireplace built into the far wall. Floor to ceiling windows with leaded lights dividing the panes of glass let in a ton of natural light, adding a bright cheerfulness to the room, giving even more charm and personality to the space. A dark, mahogany table sits in the middle, its polished surface reflecting the scene outside the windows.

"Did you need something?" Bas asked from behind me.

I glanced over my shoulder.

"No, sorry. This room is so beautiful. I was just taking it in."

"Well, there's lots to see in this house. Thankfully you have three months," he said with a smile.

I absently nodded as I fixated on the dimple that popped out in his right cheek. When I realized I was just standing there awkwardly staring at him, I shook myself out of it.

He walked past me and I followed him through the dining room and foyer, and up the curved staircase to the second floor. I walked behind him into the bedroom and looked up at the beamed ceilings and chandelier. The room is large, with a king-sized bed as well as a sitting area off to the side.

I glanced over at Bas, who was watching me expectantly.

"I'm sorry. I feel like a country bumpkin, but I've never been inside a house this beautiful. It's so elegant, I'm in awe."

He nodded.

"It's been in the family for generations." He looked around the room. "I grew up here so sometimes I forget how grand it is. It's nice when new people come in and remind me," he said with a smile. That damn dimple appeared again, but thankfully he turned serious before I got lost in it. "The loo is there and this is the closet." He pointed toward the doors in question. "I'll go see if Mum needs any help while you freshen up and whatnot."

After he left, I sat on the edge of the bed. This is all so surreal. Between flying over in my first class seat, being picked up by a handsome stranger, and now calling this amazing space home for the next three months, my head is spinning. The temptation to lie down was strong, but instead I stood and headed to the bathroom. Sharon made lunch. It would be rude to take a nap.

After freshening up, I headed back downstairs. Sharon and Bas had been in the middle of a conversation, but stopped talking when I entered the kitchen. She looked over at me and smiled.

"You have some pink in your cheeks," she said.

"I washed my face. It helped wake me up."

"Have a seat."

I pulled out the chair closest to me and sat. She said she made a light lunch, but the table is full of platters and bowls.

"This looks amazing, but you didn't have to go through so much trouble."

"It's no trouble," she said as she sat across from me. "I wasn't entirely sure of your tastes, so I've whipped up a few different options. Please, help yourself."

Bas sat at the head of the table between us. He looked at me and I realized he was waiting for me to start. I'm not sure any guys I know have manners like that.

I took a sampling of each item, even though I wasn't sure what some of them were.

"Mmm, this is delicious," I said as I finished a puff pastry with some kind of meat inside. "What's it called?"

"It's a sausage roll."

"So yummy."

I didn't think I was hungry, but ended up having seconds of most everything and then finished up with some fruit and cookies.

"Bas said he shared that he's going to show you around." I nodded at Sharon's raised brow. "I think you two will have a grand time." Her gaze shifted toward Bas then back to me. "He's been working too hard and needs a break."

"Ma, please."

"Well it's true. I want London to know I'm not just abandoning her."

"I appreciate you having me here at all. Three months is a long time. Please don't feel like you have to babysit me the entire time." A yawn escaped and I placed my hand over my mouth. "Excuse me."

"It's not babysitting. I'm genuinely happy you're here." She reached over and squeezed my hand. "We have no plans for today or tomorrow beyond possibly exploring the local town and maybe venturing to a pub or two," Sharon said. "Why don't you go relax? It's early enough that if you catch a short nap, you should be able to sleep tonight. Especially if you have a pint or two."

"A nap sounds great," I said. "Let me help you clean up first."

She waved her hands.

"I'll take care of this. You relax."

After unsuccessfully trying to get her to let me help, I made my way upstairs. I changed into leggings and a T-shirt and settled into bed, pulling the pale blue comforter up over my shoulders. I have no idea if the mattress was that comfortable or if I was just extremely tired, but I fell asleep within a matter of minutes.

———

BAS

. . .

I WALKED across the yard to the main house. I'm not sure if London is going to be too jet-lagged to do anything tonight, but decided to check just in case. If she's up for it, I figured we could just walk through Burford and go to a pub.

The kitchen was empty, but I heard voices coming from the living room so I headed in that direction. I found Mum and London seated there sipping tea and engaging in cheerful conversation. Mum glanced over at me and smiled.

"There he is. We were just wondering if you had anything planned for tonight."

I settled into the chair next to London and looked at her.

"Wasn't entirely certain if you'd be game for heading out, but just in case you're not completely worn out, I was thinking we could have a wander around the town and maybe pop into a couple of pubs.

"That sounds great," she said. "I feel totally refreshed after my nap and shower, so I'm good to go."

"Interested in joining us?" I asked mum.

"No, you two go have fun."

She didn't give a reason for not wanting to come along. Dad is away this week speaking at an academic conference, so she'll just be here alone. I can't help but wonder if Mum setting me up as London's tour guide is some sort of matchmaking scheme. If that's the case, I can't fathom what her motives could be. Not that I'd be opposed to exploring my attraction to London, but we do live on different continents so there's no chance anything between us could be long term.

A half hour later, I was guiding London through the village.

"I love this," she said. "I feel like I'm on a movie set. It's adorable."

"Burford is known as the gateway to the Cotswolds. There's actually a lot to do nearby we can add to our list."

"What kind of things?"

"Typical English countryside kind of things. River walks that pass through meadows and take you over medieval bridges and past ancient churches and manor houses. "

"It's amazing how old everything is, and it's all just right here."

"Well, not all of it, but a nice piece," I said with a smile. "Let me know if you want to stop in any of the shops here."

Up to now, we'd only walked past food-related shops, but when we approached a clothing store, she slowed down.

"Could we go in here?" she asked. "I brought a sweater, but I think it's heavier than what I'll need most days. I'd love to find a light cardigan."

"Sure."

I opened the door and shifted back for her to enter ahead of me. The shop clerk greeted London and immediately engaged her in conversation after hearing her American accent. London seemed to be in good hands, so I walked over toward the window and alternately looked out at the street and scrolled through my phone.

"All done."

"That was fast."

"Molly was very helpful. She led me to exactly what I was looking for."

After saying goodbye to the very helpful Molly, we left the stop and continued down the street to explore some more. We popped into some other shops, including a bookstore, where we stayed for quite some time. But as we continued on, the shops were closing for the night.

"One pub I have in mind is down the road and up a side street. Unless you wanted to walk around a bit more?"

"The pub sounds good. I could use a drink."

It didn't take us long to walk there and as we stepped inside, I heard familiar voices.

"Is that Bas?"

"I can't believe he's finally decided to show his face."

My eyes adjusted to the dim interior and I spotted my friends crowded around a high top in the center of the pub. Daniel, whose voice was the first I heard, came over and patted me on the back.

"It's good to see you." He shifted his gaze between London and me. "Hello," he said to her.

"Hi," she said, lifting her hand in an awkward wave.

"Let me do the introductions all at once," I said. "Everyone, this is London Spencer. She's visiting from America and staying with Mum." I pointed at each of my friends as I named them and they shook her hand in turn. "London, this is Daniel Hughes, Benji Clarke, Alex Johnson, and Davis Green."

"It's nice to meet you all," she said.

Davis pulled out a chair and smiled at London.

"Please join us."

She didn't hesitate in taking a seat and Davis settled next to her. I sat on the other side and the others filled in around the table.

"We were about to order food," Davis said. He directed that to London as he handed her a menu. "I recommend the shepherd's pie. It's my favorite meal here."

She offered a shy smile and looked at the menu. Before Davis completely took the reins, I asked if she'd like a drink.

"I'll have a beer." She looked toward the bar and frowned. "What are you having?"

"A Beavertown."

"I'll try that."

I walked over to the bar and placed our orders. While I waited, I watched London interact with my friends. I heard them ask questions about where she's from, what she's doing here, and how she knows me. She answered them politely, if a bit shyly. Davis didn't take his eyes off her the entire time, which annoyed me. Before I could analyze my reaction, the drinks were up.

"Here you go," I set the pint in front of her and sat. "Have you decided on something to eat?"

"I'm leaning toward the fish and chips," she said as she handed me the menu.

It pleased me more than it should that she didn't take Davis's suggestion and order shepherd's pie.

"I think I'll go with the burger and chips."

We all ordered food, then chatted while waiting for it to be delivered. Everyone seemed to like London and she looked more comfortable than when we'd first arrived. Davis pulled her into a side conversation and I focused on what Daniel was saying.

"Sarah will be peeved she missed you tonight," he said, referring to his fiancée. "She and Ollie went off to London to see a play."

Olivia aka Ollie used to be Sarah's roommate and is the only other female constant in our little group. Davis, Alex, Benji, and I have brought women we were dating along throughout the years, but they didn't stick around after the breakups. Which is completely understandable. Although Sarah and Ollie often complain about it. They said the group needs more estrogen.

After eating, we stayed for another pint, but then it was obvious London was tired.

"Ready to hit the road?" I asked her.

She nodded as she stifled a yawn.

"Yeah, all of a sudden I'm exhausted."

"Are you okay to walk home or would you like me to call a cab?"

Before she could answer, Davis butted in.

"I'll take you home."

London looked at me, her brow raised.

"You don't have to end your night early," I said.

"It's fine. I was going to call it a night soon anyway."

He stood and held out his hand, as if London needed help getting off of her chair. She didn't leave him hanging and put her hand in his, but I was happy to see her let it go as soon as she was on her feet.

I promised to bring London to the pub again and we all said goodbye. Davis's car was parked at the end of the block. I opened the passenger door and slid the seat forward.

"I can sit in the back," London said.

"No, I'm good. Ladies in front."

I climbed into the back, spotting the smirk on Davis's face through the rearview. London settled into the passenger seat, and we were off. It's a short ride home, so we arrived in no time.

Davis shifted into park and surprised me by getting out of the car. London had opened the door and stood just as he reached the passenger side. My stomach tightened as he leaned closer to her and said something.

Before she could answer, I sat forward and said, "Could you let me out, please?"

"Sorry about that."

London leaned down and pressed the lever. I pushed the seat forward and stepped out.

"Thanks for the ride," I said.

"Yeah, I appreciate it," London said.

"It was totally my pleasure." He looked at London. "So what else is on the agenda while you're here?"

"I'm not exactly sure. Bas is in charge of the schedule."

"Well, if you get sick of this guy, I'd be happy to show you around." He handed her a business card. "My number and email are on there. Give me a call. Anytime."

We said goodbye, and he got in the car and pulled out of the driveway.

"Thanks for tonight. I had fun."

"You're welcome," I said. "If you're up to it, I was thinking we could head to Cambridge tomorrow."

"That sounds good. What time?"

"Is noon okay?"

"I'll be ready," she said. "Well, thanks again. Goodnight."

I watched her walk across the patio and waited until the door closed behind her before heading to the carriage house.

It's odd. London and I have only had a few hours together, yet I feel a strong sense of connection to her. The possessive, protective, and jealous feelings that bubbled up when Davis was flirting with her took me off guard.

I settled onto the couch and switched on the TV and searched for something that would engage me enough to distract me from overanalyzing my emotions.

Chapter Four

"I WASN'T EXPECTING you to be awake."

My aunt's face smiled back at me from my phone screen.

"I just woke up. I'm glad I got your text before I stepped into the shower," she said. "So how's it going so far?"

"Good. Bas showed me around town last night and then we had dinner with some of his friends at a local pub."

"Bas?"

"Sharon's son. It's short for Sebastian."

I told her about how he's going to be the one escorting me to most places and why.

"Is he cute?"

She asked, drawing out the last word.

"I guess." Before she could ask another question, I

decided to change the subject. "This house is amazing. Check out this room."

I flipped the phone around and panned across my bedroom then turned it to face me again.

"Wow! That room is as big as my old apartment."

"It seriously is. I can't imagine actually living here."

"Well, it's your home for the next three months, so enjoy."

"I plan on soaking in that enormous tub later. Sharon left a welcome basket in here for me that included lavender bath salts. They smell so good."

"And what do you plan on doing before that?"

"Bas and I are heading to Cambridge shortly."

"I'm sure you'll enjoy that."

I debated on whether or not to share what I've been thinking since I left the airport. Then I decided to go for it.

"It's funny, I've never been to England before, but I feel like I belong here. I had such a sense of homecoming yesterday." Aunt Maisie stared silently at me, her face serious. "I know. It's strange."

"No it's not. Your mom always said the same thing." She offered a forced smile. "Our ancestors *are* from there. It's in your blood, I guess."

I shrugged then nodded. That was enough serious talk for today. I'm not going to get into how comfortable I already feel with Bas.

"You still need to take a shower and I have to get going. Let me give you the two-minute tour before we hang up." I grabbed my purse, slipped on shoes, and headed out of the room. "Sharon headed out to lunch with friends so the house is empty. Feel free to ooh and aah as much as you'd like," I said with a chuckle.

I walked around, panning through the empty bedrooms before heading downstairs.

"I feel like a princess every time I walk down this staircase."

"I can see why," she said.

After a quick tour of the downstairs, I went outside to show her the yard.

"Lo, it's gorgeous. You're very lucky to be staying there."

I turned the phone around to see her face again.

"It's definitely more comfortable than a hotel," I said. "I just hope I don't wear out my welcome by staying here so long."

"You're very low maintenance. I'm sure you'll be fine." She shifted her eyes to the side, then back toward me and her mouth curled into a smile. "*You guess* he's cute?"

"What?"

She dramatically moved her head to the side as if trying to look over my shoulder. I turned and saw Bas walking across the yard.

"He looks like a young Henry Cavill."

"Shhh." I faced her again. "He'll hear you."

"Hello," she said.

"Hello," Bas said from just behind me.

"Bas, this is my Aunt Maisie," I said. "Aunt Maisie, this is Sharon's son Bas."

"It's lovely to meet you," Bas said.

"Cute and good manners too." Aunt Maisie bobbed her eyebrows. "Well, I have to go get ready for work. You kids have fun today."

Before she could say anything embarrassing, I said goodbye and ended the call, promising to call again.

"You ready to go?" Bas asked, seemingly unaffected by my aunt.

Hopefully he didn't hear her Henry Cavill comment, no matter how accurate it might be.

"Let me just get my purse."

I grabbed it off the island, then headed back outside, locking the door behind me. We walked across the driveway and the garage door opened as we approached. I must have looked confused, because Bas held up his phone.

"I have an app that controls the opener."

"That's convenient."

"Very," he said. "It's a bit tight on the passenger side, so wait here while I pull the car out."

I watched him walk away, taking a second to appreciate his long, lean form and easy stride. He seems so comfortable in his own skin, which is something I both envy and appreciate. It's something I've been working on since high school.

I'd been so distracted by Bas, I hadn't noticed the car until he pulled out of the garage. I settled into the passenger seat.

"A BMW convertible?"

No wonder he hadn't brought it to the airport. If I'd had more than my two bags, they definitely wouldn't have fit. There's no back seat and the trunk can't be very large.

"It was a splurge after my first big job." Before I could ask what kind of work he does, he asked, "Would you like me to put the top down?"

"Sure."

Reaching into my purse, I grabbed a scrunchie and pulled my hair into a messy bun. By the time I was done, the top was down. The engine revved to life and Bas shifted the car into reverse and pulled out of the driveway.

"I'm surprised you're driving," I said. "I thought people took trains everywhere here."

"Public transportation is top-notch, but it's actually faster to drive to Cambridge from here." He glanced over at me and smiled. "Plus riding in a convertible on a beautiful day is its own experience."

The man wasn't lying. Between the bright sun, brilliant blue sky, and wind caressing my skin, my senses are on overdrive. And as we drove along, I felt a weight lift from my shoulders. I can't remember the last time I felt so light. Probably before mom was diagnosed more than eight years ago. Before I went down that rabbit hole and brought my mood down, I decided to find out more about Bas.

"What do you do for a living?"

"I'm a comic book artist and more recently I've started illustrating video games."

"That's impressive." I looked around the car. "I guess it's a pretty good job."

"It has been recently. More so since I started with video game illustrations."

I hadn't even thought about the fact that Bas has a job. Hopefully he's not taking time off just to spend time with me.

"If you need to work, don't worry about taking me places. Either I can amuse myself or we can work around your schedule."

"Thank you, but that's not necessary," he said. "I finished a big project last week and planned some time off. I've been working nonstop for three years now and needed a break."

That explains some of the things his friends said last night.

"I just don't want to intrude on any plans you had."

"The only plan I had was to work on my cottage and I'll still be able to do that when we're not doing anything."

"I could help." He gave me a quick glance then turned his attention back to the road as we entered a turn. "I'm not a licensed carpenter or anything, but I'm good at tearing things apart and cleaning up."

"Thank you for the generous offer."

"I'm serious. It could be a thank you for showing me around."

He didn't answer for a few seconds.

"I appreciate that," he finally said. "Maybe we'll spend rainy days scraping wallpaper and tearing up tile."

"Just give me fair warning so I can buy some work clothes."

"Now I understand the motivation behind your offer."

"What?"

"You just want to go shopping."

My stomach flipped at his teasing smile. I've done my fair share of dating, but have never felt this kind of instant attraction to someone before. It should be unsettling, but for some reason I find it exhilarating.

As we merged onto the highway, Bas turned up the radio. My heart skipped a beat then pounded as the first notes of *Stone in Love* by Journey vibrated through the speakers. It's one of my mom's favorite songs and, even though it may be a coincidence that it's playing at this moment, I can't help but feel she's with me right now, offering her approval.

BAS

WHEN MUM first asked me to be London's tour guide, I'll admit, it was the last thing I wanted to do. Yet as usual, Sharon Middleton knew best.

I've got to admit, I'm really having a good time hanging out with London, and any fretting about things getting awkward was totally uncalled for. This is our second day together and I feel like I've known her forever. Yes, there's an underlying attraction, but beyond that, I genuinely like her. She's kind, has a great sense of humor, and we're getting along really well.

"I didn't know that cemetery existed," she said. "Thank you for taking me there."

We started our day at the Cambridge American Cemetery where American soldiers who didn't make it home from World War II are buried.

"I always find being there is very powerful," I said. "It's sad to think that those graves only represent a small fraction of the people lost in the war."

She nodded and took a sip of beer, looking around the pub.

"And this place is amazing."

After walking through the campus of Cambridge, we're having a late lunch at The Eagle, the second oldest pub in the area. We've taken a seat in the back room, commonly referred to as the RAF bar.

"Supposedly this was a favorite haunt of off-duty RAF personnel during World War II." I looked up at the amber ceiling, which is completely covered with graffiti. "From what I remember, a British airman was the first to burn his squadron's number up there. Then it became tradition for airmen to add their squadron, plane, or initials."

The waitress arrived with our lunch, and there was a pause in the conversation as we tucked in. London cast her eyes around the pub, taking in all the memorabilia

"I could probably come here every day for a month and not see everything."

"You're most likely right," I said. "When my dad gets home, ask him about this place. He knows a lot about it."

She took a drink and set her glass down.

"I really like this beer."

"Do you really?" I pointed to the glass covered with colorful psychedelic skulls. "Or do you just like the glass it's served in?"

She laughed as she chewed on a chip.

"I'd say I like them equally. It's a really cool glass."

I made a mental note to purchase some she can take home with her. Then the thought of her going home made me sad so I shook it out of my head.

"When we're finished here, we're going punting."

"What's punting?"

"It's a boat that you ride along the river. Sort of like a gondola," I said. "And while we're punting along, the punter shares some history of the university and surrounding area."

"Sounds fun." She finished her beer and set the glass down. "Thank you for planning all this. I'm sure there are other things you'd rather be doing."

I shook my head.

"There's honestly nowhere I'd rather be at this moment."

Her eyes widened and the air between us crackled. I don't know how long we sat there staring into each other's eyes before the waitress returned to clear our plates. Once she left, London stood.

"I'm going to hit the ladies room," she said.

I observed her as she walked off, appreciating the distance it put between us. It will give me a minute to gather my thoughts. It's obvious she feels this attraction and I'm still not sure if we should delve into it or not. Moreover, I'm unsure how we'll avoid pursuing it when we'll be spending so much time together the next three months.

London returned and after I paid the bill, we left The

Eagle and headed toward the punt launches. She looked around, asking an occasional question. Thankfully I was able to answer.

We arrived a few minutes early for our reservation, so we stepped aside to wait.

"Do you do this often?" she asked.

"I haven't been here in probably eight years, so it's going to be a treat for me as well."

Soon enough, our punt was ready and I held her hand as she stepped in. I thought about holding onto it as I followed her in, but didn't. Once we were settled, our punter introduced himself as Brett and told us what to expect for the next hour. Then he put his pole in the water and started us on our journey along the River Cam through the College Backs.

London pulled out her phone and snapped pictures as Brett told us stories about the buildings we passed as well as local lore. She was fully engaged in the experience and asked Brett questions about most everything he said.

We were approximately three-quarters of the way down when I spotted the floating bar serving the boat behind us.

"Would you like a drink?"

She looked to where I was pointing and her eyes widened.

"There's seriously a bar on the river?"

Brett chuckled at her reaction.

"I'll take that as a yes," he said as he gestured for them to come over.

The bar sidled up next to us and we each ordered a beer, then were on our way again.

London looked so happy, I wanted to capture the moment. I pulled my phone out of my pocket and shifted closer to her.

"Let's take a selfie while the bridge is right behind us."

I held out my phone and we tilted our heads together so they were both on the screen. After clicking a few pictures, I reluctantly moved away and put my phone in my pocket.

Brett looked toward the right.

"Watch out."

He put his pole in the water and moved us to the left, but it wasn't enough. I saw the punt he'd spotted coming right at us. I put my arm around London's waist and pulled her toward me. As the boat crashed into us, I realized it wasn't enough. I dragged her across my lap, but not in time. The other boat had hit her in the side.

"Are you okay?" I asked.

Her fingers curled into my chest as she nodded.

Brett had words with the other punter as he moved away from us and continued in the other direction.

"Are you hurt?" he asked.

She shifted off me, but I kept my arm around her waist as she stayed pressed against my side.

"I'm fine."

"What a moron. He could have at least said he was sorry," he said. "Are you sure you're not hurt?'

"I'm good, thanks. It didn't hit me very hard."

It shouldn't have hit her at all, but I didn't say that out loud. What happened wasn't Brett's fault and harping on it would only ruin the rest of the ride. London said she's not hurt, which is the important thing. With my arm still around her, I forced myself to relax and enjoy the moment.

Chapter Five

LONDON

"HAVE YOU BEEN ENJOYING YOURSELF?" Sharon asked.

I'd been focused on the scenery as we drove along, thinking about how different it looks in the rain. I turned my head to look at her and smiled.

"I am. We've done so much in a week."

One of the places on my mom's list was Bath, so Bas and I went there the day after our Cambridge adventure. First stop was the Jane Austen Centre, where I delved into the life of one of my favorite authors. I enjoyed the exhibits and the costumed characters that told the story of Austen's life in the city.

Next up were the Roman Baths. I wasn't sure what to expect, but was amazed at how impressive and well-preserved the structure is. We finished the visit by climbing to the top of Abbey's Tower. Thankfully we saved that for last, otherwise I may not have made it through the other things. I was panting and sweaty by the time I reached the top, but the views of the city and surrounding countryside were worth it.

"Bath was one of the cities your mum wanted to visit."

"It was."

"I wish I'd seen her more through the years," she said. "But you get busy with life and think you have all the time in the world."

"She'd talked about coming back here for years, but couldn't swing it financially. We saved money so we could come after I graduated high school, but…" I trailed off.

"It's all right, love." Sharon squeezed my hand. "You're here now and I know she's always with you."

A gust of wind rocked the car and we swerved a little before she righted us.

"Wow." I gestured toward the windshield that the wipers were struggling to keep clear. "I guess we've been lucky with weather up to now."

"Yes, I suppose we were due for a proper downpour," she said. "Although this is a bit much."

"I'm sorry for bringing you out in this."

"You didn't bring me anywhere. I offered."

We're headed to the mall so I can get some work clothes. According to the forecast, it's going to rain the next few days so I'll make good on my offer and help Bas work at his house.

"I appreciate it."

"You know, you don't have to work on Bas's house. He's happy to show you around. You don't owe him anything for it."

"I know, but I want to help."

"Just be sure you don't hurt yourself," she said. "And also, take time to relax while you're here. Like you said, you've done a lot in a week."

Aside from Bath, we spent a lot of time exploring the Cotswolds and walked two of the trails along the River Windrush. Another day was spent in Oxford.

Before I had to answer, we arrived at the mall. Thankfully the rain had slowed a little so we're not getting out of the car and stepping into torrential downpours.

Sharon reached behind me then handed me an umbrella before pulling another from under her seat for herself.

"Here we go," she said with a smile.

I cracked the door open just far enough to pop the umbrella out and opened it. We jogged through the parking lot and by the time we stepped through the automatic doors, my feet and ankles were soaked.

"What kind of clothes would you like?" she asked as we set our umbrellas in the stand.

"Something I can get dirty. Leggings, jeans, T-shirts."

She took me to a store that reminded me of TJ Maxx back home. We headed to the women's section and sorted through the racks. Before long, I had an armful of things to try on. I don't need much. It's not like I'll be working on his house forty hours a week.

Everything fit, but I restrained myself and only bought a pair of jeans and two pair of leggings. But my restraint didn't apply to the shirts. Sharon had found five retro band T-shirts, which are my weakness. And, while I already have a couple of the bands, they're all designs I don't own. I couldn't decide which ones to put back so I took them all. So I'll be adding Queen, the Rolling Stones, Journey, Fleetwood Mac, and Def Leppard to the ones I already own.

"It's a good thing I brought an extra piece of luggage," I said to Sharon as I collected my bags. "Aunt Maisie will be proud that I bought something for myself. Granted these are things I may be able to find at home, but I'll remember where they're from and that makes them special."

"What else do you need?"

"Nothing." I held up my bags. "This is it."

"I don't think I've ever had such a speedy trip to the mall."

"We lucked out and found what I needed right away."

We walked back toward the entrance, collected our umbrellas, and headed to the car.

"I mentioned to Bas that we'd get him some lunch as I drop you off. There's a sandwich place not too distant from here. We can have a quick bite and also grab something for him."

A few minutes later she parked on the street and turned off the car. I looked around at yet another area of quaint old buildings.

"Everything here looks so classic. I keep telling Bas I feel like I'm on a movie set half the time."

"England is old."

"It's just amazing that these buildings are still standing and in good enough shape to be utilized."

We got out of the car and I followed her into what I'd refer to as a deli. My mouth watered at the familiar smells. I followed Sharon to a table near the window and the waitress immediately approached with menus.

"Can I get you ladies something to drink?" she asked.

"Coke," Sharon said.

"I'll have a Coke, too."

"Let me fetch those and I'll be back for your orders."

"Is anything catching your eye?" Sharon asked.

"You know, I was thinking ham and cheese. But I've been trying to eat things I can't get at home," I said. "What are you having?"

"Egg and cress."

I looked at that and while I do like egg salad, I'm not sure now is the time to eat it. Sometimes eggs bother my stomach and I don't want to have issues while I'm working with Bas.

"I think I'll go with the coronation chicken sandwich." I set my menu down and looked over at her. "That looks different enough from chicken salad to count."

The waitress returned with our drinks and took our orders, including a ham and cheese sandwich to go for Bas. When she left, Sharon looked at me and smiled.

"We'll pick up an assortment of biscuits at the bakery next door, too. Bas has quite a sweet tooth."

Our food arrived within minutes of ordering. Sharon's phone buzzed just as we were about to dig in.

"Pardon me," she said. "It's my daughter."

I looked out the window as I picked up my sandwich and took a bite. I'm happy with my choice. Its texture is the same as chicken salad, but the sweet, savory flavor is different.

"I apologize." Sharon's voice pulled my attention back to her. "She never rings, so when she does, I worry that it's an emergency."

"Is everything okay?"

"It is. She just called to tell me she'll be home for the weekend." Her eyes widened. "We'd planned to go for tea. We'll do that while she's here."

Sharon told me about Elsie while we finished lunch. She seems to think we'll have a lot in common. Either way, it will be nice to get to know her.

After I practically wrestled her for the check, I pulled out my credit card and paid.

"You really didn't have to do that, but thank you." She got up, smiling. "Now, shall we go find some lovely sweets?"

. . .

BAS

I HEARD the front door close a second before a voice echoed up the stairs.

"Hello?"

"Be right down."

After washing my hands, I headed downstairs. London stood in the foyer, holding a pink pastry box in one hand and a white bag in the other. She held both up as I approached.

"Lunch has arrived."

"Thank you," I said and took the items from her and walked to the kitchen. "Don't mind the mess. I've been tearing things apart when I have time. Unfortunately putting them back together is a much slower process."

"When you said you have a cottage, I anticipated something much smaller than this." She looked around the kitchen. "But this is a nice size."

"I inherited this from the same people who gave my parents their house, so to them, this is small."

"Ah, that explains it." She looked around. "I guess it's all relative."

"Have a seat." I set the bag and box on the table. "Would you like a drink?" I opened the refrigerator. "I have beer or water."

"I'll have water."

I grabbed two bottles and sat across from her.

"This is perfect timing. My stomach just started growling." Opening the bag, I pulled out the sandwich and crisps. "How was shopping?"

"Good. I found what I needed almost immediately."

She waved her hand down then up her body. "Nothing but the best attire to work at Chez Bas."

I glanced down at my ripped jeans and stained T-shirt before meeting her gaze again.

"I appreciate you're respecting my strict dress code."

Her answering chuckle warmed my heart. When I first picked London up at the airport,

two words I would have used to describe her would be polite and serious. Now she's more animated and quick to laugh. She also has an inner glow that wasn't there before.

I unwrapped my sandwich and took a big bite, then opened the crisps while I chewed.

London and I have spent a lot of time together this past week and there've been a lot of lingering stares and almost kisses. But something always interrupted before anything happened.

Before I could analyze things further, she said, "Oh, I almost forgot. Your mom wanted me to tell you that your sister is coming home this weekend. She's making reservations for tea Saturday, but she wants to have a family dinner Sunday."

"So between the rain and Elsie's visit, it looks like we won't be venturing out until next week." I finished half of the sandwich and took a drink. "I was planning on shooting her a message this week to see when would be a good time for us to head to London. Her flat's right in South Bank, and she's kindly offered us a few days to crash while we do all the touristy things. But I'll just wait to speak to her in person."

"It's funny. When I thought about coming here, all I pictured was the countryside. The city didn't even enter my mind."

"If you want the complete British experience, London is a must. Especially since it's your namesake." I finished the sandwich and crisps, put the empty wrappers in the bag, and set it aside. "What did mum get at the bakery?"

"I'm not even sure," London said. "Dodger jaffy something."

I pulled the pink box toward me and opened it. The sweet smell made my mouth water.

"Jaffa cake, jammie dodgers, bourbon biscuits, and sticky toffee pudding." I looked at her. "Odd. That last one isn't something I normally eat."

"That's for me," she said. "I mentioned that I love caramel and she told me I had to taste it."

She looked in the box.

"Are the jammie dodgers the cookies I had at your mom's my first day here?"

"They are."

"I like those. We call them linzer cookies back home, but I like your name better. It's cute."

"I don't have any plates here, but I do have a fork."

I walked over to the counter, snagged a pack of plasticware, and handed it to her. She

popped out the fork and dug into the pudding.

"Mmm, this is so good."

My cock stood at attention at her orgasmic sounds. I reached for a Jaffa cake, shoved it in my mouth, and chewed. The sight of her licking toffee off her fork didn't do anything to calm my libido. I stared at the table and finished the cake, then reached for a bourbon biscuit. My theory is that if I concentrate on eating, maybe it'll distract me from what she's doing. The problem is, I can't keep my eyes from shifting in her direction or stop from hearing her sexy sounds.

"When I hear toffee, I think of something hard, but this is just caramel."

My something hard is becoming very uncomfortable.

She took another bite and let out a long moan. If she was any other woman, I'd think she's doing it on purpose. But this is London. She's genuinely just enjoying the cake. And driving me crazy in the process.

"I can't take another bite."

She leaned back in the chair and rested her hand against her stomach. I looked over and spotted a dot of toffee just above her top lip. Closing my eyes, I struggled to muster up more control, but seem to be out. Opening them again, I zeroed on the toffee and stood.

London's eyes widened as I stepped toward her, rested my hands on the arms of the chair, and leaned down.

"You have toffee on your lip."

Her tongue darted out, but the toffee stayed firmly in place, taunting me.

"Want me to give it a try?" I said.

The corners of her mouth curled up just the slightest bit and she slowly nodded. I didn't need more of an invitation than that. I leaned closer still until we were a mere breath apart and licked at her top lip. Toffee has never really been my thing, but starting now, it's going to top my list of favorite sweets.

I pulled back and admired my handiwork just a second before pressing my mouth against hers. I'd meant to just brush my lips against hers once or twice to get it out of my system, but it quickly turned into something else. The powerful kiss had me craving more and without releasing her mouth, I lifted her out of the chair, sat her on the table, and stepped between her wide-spread thighs.

Sliding my hands down to cup her ass, I pulled her against me and opened my mouth over hers to deepen the kiss. She threaded her fingers through my hair as our tongues tangled together. Sticky toffee pudding lingered on her palette, but as the kiss went on, I finally got to taste her. She's just as delicious as the baked goods.

I dragged my hand along her thigh, stopping to squeeze her hip before moving up and dipping my fingers under the hem of her shirt. With my palm flat against her waist, my thumb rested just under the edge of her bra.

The kiss went on, long and hot and sweet. Through her bra, I rubbed my thumb back and forth over her hard nipple, and an answering moan vibrated against my chest. I wanted more.

I squeezed and kneaded her plump breast as the kiss turned hotter and a bit desperate. She dug her fingertips into my scalp when I pinched her nipple between my thumb and forefinger. At least I know I'm not the only one affected here.

My cock throbbed against my zipper as we continued to snog like horny teens. I moved to press into her in an attempt to alleviate the ache when I heard a howling and a loud rattling. I jumped back and almost fell on my ass. As I caught myself, I realized it was just the wind and rain.

I looked at London and found her watching me.

Stepping forward, I placed a kiss against the corner of her mouth, then I pulled back just enough to see her face. With her eyes still closed, she let out a soft hum as her swollen lips curved into a small smile.

Chapter Six

LONDON

BAS JUST STARED AT ME. I'm not sure what he's thinking and uncertainty creeped in with each passing second. Maybe he doesn't want to take this further.

I'm not sure if I said that last sentence out loud or if he just read it in my eyes, but his answer erased any doubts in my mind.

"Not here. Not the first time anyway." His crooked smile was sexy, seductive, and somewhat wicked. "I want to stretch you out on my bed and love every inch of you." His eyes glowed in the dim light and I shivered in anticipation. "Will you let me?"

The word yes had barely left my mouth when Bas took my hand and led me upstairs. We walked into a darkened room and as he turned on the bedside lamp, a soft glow filled the space.

While the rest of the house is cluttered with tools, materials, and debris, this room is a place of timelessness and serenity. The half-paneled walls and beamed ceilings combined with the elegant luster of the gold paint give the room a cozy feel.

"This room is beautiful." I focused on the four-poster bed with its intricately-carved headboard that dominated the space. "And that's amazing."

"The other rooms were wallpapered and updated to various degrees, but for some reason they left this one alone. And I really like it as is. I plan on renovating the other rooms to look like this." He nodded toward the bed. "I moved all the other furniture into storage, but kept that here on the off chance I need it." He tucked a stray hair behind my ear and offered a sweet smile. "Like when a beautiful woman travels here from the States and catches my eye."

"Does that happen often?" I asked, in what I hoped was a flirtatious tone.

He slowly shook his head.

"I'd say it's a once–in-a-lifetime experience." He stepped closer and placed his hands on either side of my face. His thumbs lightly stroked my cheeks, and even that innocent action sent erotic shivers down my spine.

"Are you sure about this?"

"I'm sure."

"Me too," he said, before crushing his mouth to mine.

His hands moved down my body, then back up, dragging my T-shirt with them. The kiss ended so he could pull it over my head. He then opened the button fly of my jeans and with expert care, dragged them down my legs.

Lying me down in the center of the bed, his gaze toured my body. I'm not normally a sexy underwear kind of girl, but my cotton set is from Victoria's Secret so it's still super cute.

"You're truly beautiful. Absolutely perfect." His fingertips brushed my abdomen. "Soft."

I'm not a virgin, but my past sexual encounters haven't exactly been Earth-shattering. Something tells me being with Bas is going to be different.

He leaned down to kiss my stomach, nipping at my navel before continuing upward. Through the fabric of my bra, he teased one nipple with his tongue, tantalizing, drawing it into the moist heat of his mouth, creating a stiff peak. His hand teased my other breast, plucking at its distended nipple. My back arched and I didn't recognize the low moan that escaped my mouth.

Releasing my right breast, he moved onto the left. Our eyes held as he ran his tongue around it ever so slowly, spiraling toward my nipple. His cheeks hollowed as he sucked.

"Bas." His name came out more as a sigh than a word.

"Hmm?" he muttered, creating delicious vibrations against my sensitized skin.

Goosebumps cascaded down my body and I forgot what I was going to say.

His fingers fumbled with the fastener of my bra, but the bed hindered his efforts. I shifted to give him more room, but it wasn't enough.

Bas backed away and cool air brushed the flesh his warm mouth vacated. He held out his hand, urging me to sit. I complied and he reached around and unhooked the bra, placing a gentle kiss on my shoulder in the process.

When he moved back, I clutched the hem of his T-shirt and lifted it, exposing a pretty impressive six pack. He removed his shirt, then threw it on the floor. I placed my hands against his abdomen and trailed my fingers up to his chest. But before I could explore, he tilted my face up and proceeded to kiss me senseless.

As promised, Bas loved every inch of me. He nuzzled my breasts before moving up and nibbling on a particularly sensitive spot just above my collarbone. Back to my breasts where he sucked my nipples to tight, achy peaks until I begged for his next touch. His hot mouth skimmed down my stomach and nibbled at my navel, dipping his tongue inside, making me squirm.

He hooked his fingers beneath the waistband of my underwear and pulled them slowly down my legs then tossed them on the floor. After kissing my knee, he dragged his mouth back up and settled between my thighs.

When he placed an open-mouthed kiss at their juncture, I nearly jumped off the bed. Bas pressed a restraining hand against my belly as his gaze met mine over the expanse of my body. He continued his sensual torture, licking and nipping and sucking until I didn't think I could take anymore. When his tongue slid over the tiny nub of nerves, I gasped and squeezed my fingers into his dark hair.

He stopped what he was doing and glanced up.

"Did I hurt you?" he asked.

"No." My chuckle came out as more of a moan. "It just feels so good."

I caught a glimpse of his devilish smile as he bent, once again, to the task at hand.

Bas slipped his middle finger into my slick folds and began a steady in and out motion while his tongue teased my clit. I arched toward him, my breath coming in shallow pants. His index finger joined in the game and the rhythm increased, sending ripples of sensation through my entire body.

I was so close to something I've never fully experienced before and Bas seemed intent on making me lose my mind. He shifted and trailed a path of kisses up my stomach and to my breasts, never once removing his hand from between my thighs.

The man is a master of multi-tasking. Two fingers pumped while his thumb circled my engorged nub. As if that weren't enough, he alternately sucked one nipple then the other in time with his talented hand.

It was too much. Way too much.

I dug my fingers into his shoulders and lifted my hips. My senses swirled as all the stimuli concentrated in that magic spot then seemed to burst through my entire body. He pulled back just long enough to slide on a condom.

I'd barely recovered when Bas shifted between my thighs, plunged inside, and held himself completely still.

"London," he said, his voice a mere rasp in my ear.

We stayed like that for several heartbeats before he finally started to move. He pumped in and out, slowly at first, but gradually picked up the pace.

I felt that now-familiar tingling deep inside again and I pulsed my hips up to meet his every thrust, chasing the ultimate sensation.

It wasn't enough.

Wanting to feel more, *needing* to feel more, I wrapped my legs around his waist.

That did it. His next thrusts had him hitting the perfect spot. It didn't take a lot for me to completely shatter. I let out a long, hoarse moan as I came for the second time in less than five minutes. Some part of my brain registered the fact that Bas had let out his own shout just before he collapsed on top of me.

———

BAS

I pushed open the door of my parents' house, feeling

the warmth from the kitchen wrap around me. The familiar smell of Sunday roast filled the air and my stomach growled in anticipation.

London stood next to mum at the stove stirring gravy. Without stopping, she turned her head and smiled at me.

"Oh good, you're here," Mum said. "You can help your sister set the table."

I'm not surprised by her lack of a warm greeting. When Mum hosts any sort of gathering, she gets very militant. Even if it's just a family dinner. Elsie and I have termed it *party mode.*

"I've done it." Elsie punched my arm as she walked past. "Whilst you were sleeping in, the womenfolk were slaving away in the kitchen to feed you."

"I wasn't sleeping in," I said. "I was slaving away at the cottage."

Even though London and I have spent the past week at the cottage, we didn't get any work done. Instead, we spent the days in bed, exploring each other's bodies and getting to know one another on a deeper level.

"Enough chatting," mum said. "Bas, go tell your father we're eating shortly."

"I'll tell him," Elsie said. "I'm going up anyway."

"Don't get lost up there," Mum said.

Elsie looked at me and rolled her eyes then mouthed *party mode.* I chuckled, then shook my head and shrugged.

"I think this is done," London said, still stirring.

I've worked as Mum's assistant and I'm certain she's under strict instructions to not stop until the gravy is properly thickened.

"Almost there. Give it another minute." Mum reached for oven gloves and slipped them on. "Shift to the side dear, so you don't get burned."

London moved away from the stove. Mum reached

inside, pulled out the pan, and placed it on the trivet she'd set on the counter. The scent of roast chicken grew more intense and my stomach gave a hungry grumble.

As she usually does, Mum instructed all of us to go take our seats in the dining room. She'll organize the chicken, potato, and veg on a platter and bring it in. She likes to make a grand presentation.

London washed and dried her hands, then I followed her into the dining room. Dad and Elsie haven't come downstairs yet, so I took the opportunity to give London a kiss. I haven't seen her for almost two days and it feels like an eternity.

"I missed you."

Before she could respond, I heard dad and Elsie walking down the stairs. I gave London one more quick kiss and stepped back. We haven't told anyone we're together. I don't normally introduce women I'm dating to my family in the early stages, and there's no reason to do it now.

Dad, Elsie, and I settled into our usual seats at the table and I gestured for London to sit next to me.

"What's on your agenda this week?" Dad asked.

"Possibly Stratford-upon-Avon," I said.

"You'll enjoy Tudor World," he said to London. "It's an interactive living history museum."

As he regaled her with Shakespearean facts, I thought about asking him to join us. He showed us around Oxford and London enjoyed his company and all the historical tidbits he shared. If Mum comes along, it would be like a double date. Even if they're unaware that's what it is.

Mum glided into the room, platter in hand. She takes pride in her presentations of Sunday roast so we fussed over the artful display. After setting the feast down, she ran back to the kitchen and returned with a plate of Yorkshire pudding. She set it on the table and took her seat.

"Enjoy," she said. "I'd like to extend my thanks to London, who took charge of the gravy today. It's bound to be a treat since she actually paid heed to my instructions."

London's cheeks pinked adorably at the faint praise and I resisted the urge to lean closer and kiss her.

We passed around the platter and each filled our plates with chicken, roast potatoes, parsnips, and carrots. When London took a Yorkshire pudding, she chuckled.

"When your mom said we were making Yorkshire pudding, I was expecting a dessert item like Jell-O pudding we have in the US or the sticky toffee pudding I had last week."

London's eyes rounded and she looked at me. Memories flowed between us of what happened directly after she ate her sticky toffee pudding.

"I believe Americans call these popovers."

Dad's words broke the spell between London and me.

"Yes," she said. "Popovers."

"And that's why George Bernard Shaw observed that the British and Americans are two great peoples divided by a common tongue."

We all chuckled at that, then concentrated on eating. I was glad for the break. Thoughts of our first night together put me in a state I don't necessarily want to be in surrounded by family.

"The meal is delicious as always, my dear."

My dad is right about that. Mum is an excellent cook, and a master at the Sunday roast. The chicken is cooked to perfection and its accompanying vegetables crisp and flavorful. I'd covered both with the gravy London had stirred to perfect thickness.

"Bas, I looked at my calendar, and anytime after this week works for me," Elsie said.

I'd been so caught up in London's blush that it took a second to register what she was actually talking about.

"Oh, brilliant. We'll take it as it comes, depending on the weather," I said.

"How long do you plan on staying?" she asked. "Not that it matters. You're welcome to as long as you like. I'm just curious."

"Three or four days," I said. "That should give us enough time to see everything on London's list and then some."

"London in London," Elsie said, looking inordinately pleased with herself for making that observation.

"Do you plan on taking the train in?" Mum asked.

I nodded as I finished chewing.

"I think so. Aside from the fact it will save me the hassle of parking in the city, it'll be a new experience for London." I looked at her. "We've been driving everywhere so you haven't had a chance to experience our top-notch public transportation system."

"That sounds like fun. I've never really been on a train."

"Really?" I asked.

"Well, aside from at amusement parks or a tour kind of thing. I've never been on one for transport."

"Then I'm glad you'll get to experience it here for the first time."

I held London's gaze and smiled.

"Just give me notice before you'll be arriving," Elsie said, pulling my attention back to her. "I'll need a chance to straighten up the spare bedroom."

"Will do," I said.

"And you'll be happy to know there's a proper bed in

there now. There's also a new sofa bed in the living room, but I don't imagine you'll be using that." I raised my brow. "I just assumed you'd want to share a room."

My jaw tightened and if looks could kill, Elsie would be face down on the dining room floor. How the hell does she know?

"Whyever would they want to share a room?" Mum asked, looking between my sister and me.

Elsie shrugged.

"I thought it was obvious Bas and London are…a couple."

I'm guessing her pause is due to the fact that she was searching for something to say besides *fucking.* Mum isn't a prude and all sorts of words have been spoken in this house, but she doesn't tolerate bad language at the dinner table.

"Is that true?"

I couldn't tell if she was happy about the prospect or not, but I suppose it really doesn't matter.

London looked over at me and nibbled at her bottom lip. I gave her a small smile and shrugged, then without looking away from her answered my mum's question.

"Yes, it's true."

"Well then," she said. "It's fortunate I made both an apple crumble and Victoria sponge. It seems we're celebrating more than just a family gathering today."

Chapter Seven

I STOOD on the sidelines watching Bas play cricket. I'm not a huge baseball fan, but I have been to games and can follow what's going on. But I have no idea what's happening on this field. Sebastian had tried to explain the rules, but I found it very confusing. There doesn't appear to be a strike zone and Bas's friend Daniel got "dismissed" and I had no idea why. Sebastian said it was because of the *leg before wicket* rule. That didn't make sense to me because the ball had hit Daniel in the arm, but I didn't ask him to clarify.

"We're headed back to the house," Sharon said. "Those clouds aren't sitting right with me."

She pointed toward the dark sky that had been slowly creeping in our direction since the game started. The field is a short walk from their house, and it felt nice to get out and move after dinner. It's so different from home where we drive even the shortest of distances.

"Shall I swing back around with umbrellas?" Sebastian asked.

I looked at Elsie.

"Nah, we'll be fine. A little rain never hurt."

"Oh to be young," Sharon said. "I hate getting drenched."

"Well then, we should probably be going, my dear," Sebastian said. "The rain isn't far off."

We said goodbye and they walked off toward the path leading to their house. I turned my attention back to the game just in time to see Bas dive and catch the ball. Some of the crowd cheered and I followed Elsie's lead and clapped. His teammates high-fived and chest bumped, so I guess it was a big play in the game. At this point, I don't have a clue.

"Do you understand this game?" I asked Elsie.

"The main points." She shrugged. "People think it's like baseball, but it's not at all."

A fat drop of rain landed on my forehead and I looked up at the dark sky.

"Do you think the game will be over before the rain starts?"

"Probably not."

Thankfully I wore my hair in a braid today so it won't be a total mess if we end up walking to the pub in a deluge.

"So you and Bas," Elsie said with a sly grin.

"Yeah."

Even though we've been at it for a week, it still feels strange for me to admit it. Until now, we've been in our own little bubble.

"How's that going?"

"It's good." I shifted to better face her. "How did you know?"

"That you two are shagging?" I nodded. "You looked like you just had a good going over when I arrived Friday. Then Saturday at tea, I saw texts coming through from him. Why else would he be texting you all day? So I suspected something was happening." She shrugged. "When you kept eye fucking each other today, I knew for sure."

"Do you think your parents are upset?"

"Why would they be?"

"I don't know. I'm staying at their house…" I trailed off, not knowing what other reason to give.

"Mum didn't utter a word to me, but I reckon she's genuinely pleased," she said. "She likes you."

Bas and I are both adults, but I feel like it's going to be strange now that his parents know. I don't want to be disrespectful to them. I thought about asking Elsie how she thinks we should navigate the situation, but decided to just speak to Bas instead.

More drops fell and the game ended just as a steady drizzle began to fall. Bas was on the field for what seemed like forever with his teammates and the team they'd been playing. But finally, he came walking over with Daniel and Alex.

"What'd you think?" he asked after giving me a quick kiss.

"I enjoyed watching even though I didn't have a clue of what was going on."

"Instead of chatting here in the rain," Daniel said. "Why don't we head to the pub?"

We started walking, all of us talking and laughing. The rain got progressively heavier and we were still a block away from the pub when it started to pour. We looked at each other, then started running, laughing as we went.

By the time we burst through the door of the pub, we

were all soaked. Benji and Davis clapped as we walked toward them.

"Well done," Davis said. "Hello again." Those two words were directed at me.

"Hi."

I kept my tone light and friendly, hoping it would offset his more flirtatious one. Bas stepped up behind me and placed his hands on my waist. Davis's gaze shifted from me to a space above my head.

"So that's how it is," he said.

"It is," Bas said.

"All right then." Davis raised his pint. "Cheers to you."

Now we've outed ourselves to Bas's family and his friends. Aunt Maisie knew after our first night together. The only thing that would make it more official is if I posted it on social media.

With my wet hair and clothes, I should have been itching to go back to the house. But as Bas handed me a pint of Beavertown, I settled at the table and picked up the menu, ready to hang out for the night.

"It was cracking with you at cricket again," Daniel said. "Hopefully you'll keep coming."

"I'll try my best."

"Don't try, *do*," Benji added.

Daniel's fiancée Sarah and her friend Ollie arrived and welcomed me into the group with a warmth and openness I hadn't been expecting. When I first landed, I felt a connection with the country. Now, after spending time with Bas, his family, and friends, I feel a sense of belonging that I haven't experienced in years. Not since my mom got diagnosed with cancer and rocked my whole world.

I looked around the table and smiled as the lightness and warmth in the room settled in my chest. I'll miss this when I have to leave, but instead of focusing on that, I'm going to make it a point to enjoy every moment while I'm here.

———

BAS

Elsie and Benji stayed tucked in a corner of the pub, heads pressed together most of the night. So I wasn't surprised when she told me she was leaving with him instead of walking home with London and me.

The rest of us stayed until last call and didn't head out into the night until the bartender escorted us out the door. We stepped outside and said our goodbyes. I reached for London's hand and we headed toward home.

"So Elsie and Benji."

She raised her voice at the end of the sentence turning it into a question.

"Yeah, they dated for a bit before she moved to London." I shrugged. "I've no idea what's happening between them now."

"Was it weird having your sister and friend date?"

"I tried not to think about it too much."

"Understandable."

The rain had mostly stopped, but a light mist remained, leaving us soaked once again by

the time we reached home. We walked up the driveway and London turned toward the big house. I held onto her hand stopping her progress. She turned to face me.

I nodded my head toward the other side of the yard.

"You've been here a fortnight and still haven't seen the carriage house."

"Is that an invitation?"

"That's a permanent invitation."

With a smile, she nodded and we walked across the yard. I opened the door and stepped aside for her to enter.

"Bas, this is really nice."

I looked around the space, seeing it through her eyes. The kitchen, living, and dining areas are all one big room. It's old, but more classic than outdated. My bedroom is off to the right and London stepped inside to explore. I followed her inside, taking the opportunity to plug my dying phone into the charging station on the nightstand.

"Is that where you always work or do you go into an office?"

She pointed at the drafting table tucked into the corner of the room.

"If I'm drawing on paper, I work at the table. But when I use my iPad to create digital designs, I can do that anywhere. I rarely go into an office for more than kickoff or status meetings."

"You drew these?"

I walked up behind her.

"Those are the initial sketches I made for my last project. The final design ended up being a lot different though."

"They're amazing. I can't draw a straight line with a ruler." She looked at me and smiled. "I don't recall every detail of your visit to the States all those years ago, but I do remember that you always had your nose in a comic book. Little did I know it was research for your future career."

"Yeah, Mum was always yelling at me to get my nose out of a book and shooing me outside."

I leaned down and gave her what was supposed to be a quick kiss. Instead, I ended up crushing my mouth against hers, and we feasted on each other, our lips and tongues stroking, tasting, and savoring, as we gave in to the hunger we'd kept at bay all day. Moving my hands down her body, then back up, I removed her sopping T-shirt and ended the kiss just long enough to pull it over her head and drop it on the floor. Her soggy bra followed suit.

This past week, sex between us has run the gamut between fast and frenzied to slow and languid. Based on the way London is clawing at my shirt, tonight is going to be the former. Not that I'm complaining. No matter how we do it, it's amazing.

We ended the kiss again while she pulled off my shirt, and I took the opportunity to remove the rest of our clothes.

I shifted my hands over her ass to her hips and lifted. She wrapped her legs around my waist and I carried her across the room and sat on the edge of the bed. London straddled my lap and shifted forward until my throbbing cock pressed against heaven.

Dipping my head, I sucked her nipples into tight peaks. She twisted her fingers into my hair while her hips pulsed forward, driving me crazy.

"Bas."

I released her nipple with a soft pop and looked into her eyes. She moved her hands down to my shoulders, shifted up on her knees, and without warning, sank down onto my hard cock.

"*Christ.*"

We stopped using condoms a couple days ago, and sliding into her wet heat with no barrier is one of the most transcendent things I've ever experienced.

London groaned my name as she moved forward and back, eroding my self-control with each slow stroke. She picked up the pace I cupped her ass and squeezed, pulling her tight on each forward thrust so her clit rubbed against me.

She panted my name then opened her mouth over

mine, kissing me, our tongues thrusting in the same rhythm as her hips. Her groans got louder, her movements more and more frantic. I felt tiny ripples at the tip of my cock a mere second before she pulled back and took a deep breath before letting it out on a long, low groan. I thrust up, moving my hips in time with hers and followed her over the edge.

When our heartbeats slowed and our bodies cooled, I shifted her off me and we moved up toward the pillows and settled into bed properly. I pulled the covers up over her shoulders as she rested her head against my chest.

"I don't want to leave here," she said in a groggy voice.

"You don't have to."

"But shouldn't I go to the big house to sleep?"

"Not if you don't want to."

"Your mom won't mind?"

"I'll send her a quick text and let her know you're here so she doesn't worry."

I reached for my phone and did just that. The fact that Mum loved the text immediately eased London's worry.

It's been a long day and I'm knackered. Based on London's slow, steady breaths, I guess she was too. After pressing a kiss on her forehead, I shifted my head to rest more comfortably against my pillow and closed my eyes. My mouth curled into a small smile as I drifted off to sleep with the thought of waking next to London in the morning.

Chapter Eight

LONDON

THE PAST FEW weeks have been beyond amazing. Bas and I visited Stratford-upon-Avon and immersed ourselves in Shakespeare. Sharon and Sebastian accompanied us to Kent, where we explored the White Cliffs of Dover and Canterbury Castle, then ended the day at a winery where we enjoyed dinner and a sampling of beverages.

Today, Bas and I are taking the train to London. Sharon dropped us off at the station and we talked about our itinerary as we waited.

"I'm sorry. You're probably going to hate doing all these touristy things."

"No I won't, because I'll be doing them with you."

His adorable smile melted my heart. I know I'm staring at him like a love-struck fool, but I don't care. I can't help it. It seems too soon to exchange those three little words, but I'm definitely feeling them. Before I slip and say something I'm not ready to reveal, I blinked and broke the spell.

"I don't really care if I go on a tour of Buckingham Palace, but I would like to see the changing of the guard."

"Are you going to be one of those silly Americans that tries to break them?"

"Would you be embarrassed?"

"Of you?" He leaned forward and kissed me. "Never."

"You're very sweet."

"I'm glad you think so." An announcement sounded and he looked up at the board. "Here comes our train."

He stood and grabbed both of our bags.

"I can carry my bag."

"So can I."

The train approached and then stopped. As the doors opened, we waited for people to get off before stepping inside. I followed him down the aisle past a bunch of empty seats. When he stopped, I realized he'd been looking for two rows of seats facing each other. I settled into the seat next to the window and he sat on the other side, next to the aisle. That way our knees didn't bump. It also gave me the opportunity to rest my feet on the seat across from me and stretch my legs.

"Where is Elsie's flat located again?"

"South Bank," he said. "So a lot of places you want to go are within walking distance. We can either take the tube or a taxi to the things farther out."

I opened my phone to Google South Bank, but before I did, Aunt Maisie's face filled my screen.

"Aunt Maisie is FaceTiming me."

"Aren't you going to answer?"

"I don't want to be the rude American talking on the phone in the tube."

"There's no one around us."

I glanced around and realized he's right.

"Hi Aunt Maisie."

"Sorry I missed your call earlier," she said. "I was in the shower." Her eyes shifted to the side then looked back at me again. "Are you on a plane?"

"No, a train. Bas and I are going to London for a few days."

"Ooh, nice."

Bas shifted to the seat next to me and said, "Hi Aunt Maisie."

"Hi Bas. Are you showing my girl a good time?"

She knows what's been going on between Bas and me so that question definitely had a double meaning. Bas has been around for a few of our calls, so they've already spoken, so he knows how she is.

"I'm doing my best," he said.

"I'm sure you are," she said, bobbing her eyebrows.

I can't believe I'm sitting here on a train with Bas basically telling my aunt he's fucking me senseless every night and she's telling him she's happy about it. What bizarro world has this train driven me into?

"So what's going on at home?" I asked, trying to get the conversation back on track.

"The usual. Work and chasing Ava around," she said. "Grandma plans on coming up to visit when you get back. She wants to travel before it gets cold." She used air quotes on those last four words. "Now that she's fully immersed in St. Pete, her idea of cold has drastically changed. Apparently she won't come up North outside of May through September. She said if we want to see her at Christmas, we have to go down there. And who wants to celebrate Christmas when it's eighty degrees?" She shook her head. "But enough of my whining. You two enjoy your train ride and London." Her eyes shifted between Bas and me. "And whatever else you might be doing."

I rolled my eyes and decided to end the call before she says something really embarrassing.

"I'll talk to you later," I said. "Love you."

"I love you more," she said. "Bye Bas."

"Cheerio," he said, exaggerating his accent.

Her answering chuckle filled the air until the call ended.

"You don't have to encourage her, you know."

"Of course I do. She's fun."

Instead of moving across the way, he stayed in the seat next to me.

"That she is."

"Your gram obviously triggered her."

"All the time," I said. "My grandmother doesn't fit the stereotype of the family matriarch who makes you cookies and lives for you to visit."

"No?" I shook my head. "What's she like?"

"She's not exactly narcissistic, but she definitely thinks her family's lives should revolve around her. From what I understand, my grandfather fed that beast so others didn't have to, but once he died, the burden fell to Aunt Maisie and to a lesser degree, my mom."

"When did she move to Florida?"

"She started doing the snowbird thing about ten years ago. Her visits there got longer and she finally moved full-time five years ago when she remarried."

I don't want this trip to start with a negative tone, so I didn't mention that we're not very close. Or how I still harbor anger toward her because she didn't seem to care when my mom got sick.

"If it makes you feel any better, my grandparents aren't exactly warm and fuzzy either," he said. "But as they're British, I suppose they're not expected to be," he added with a chuckle.

"Well, you're British, and I find you very warm…" I brushed my fingers against the hair peeking out of the open buttons of his shirt. "And fuzzy."

He leaned forward and kissed me. Not just a quick brushing of the lips, but a proper kiss, complete with tongue. By the time he released me, my head was spinning and I rested it against the back of the seat. He interlaced our fingers and gave the back of my hand a kiss before setting our joined hands between us.

Sometimes I have to pinch myself to prove I'm not dreaming. This whole trip has been like a fairytale, complete with my own handsome prince. Unfortunately, this isn't going to last. Three months seemed like forever when I was boarding the plane, but now it's going by way too fast.

But instead of going down that rabbit hole of despair, once again, I reminded myself to live in the moment. Turning my head, I looked out the window and enjoyed the scenery.

———

BAS

I'VE BEEN to the city more times than I can count, but seeing it through London's eyes has made it all brand new. We've had three whirlwind days, and have spent them exploring every inch of the city. My Apple watch keeps applauding me because my step count has been so high. It's going to be disappointed once we get home and I get back to my normal routine.

Tonight is our last in the city and I booked a Thames

dinner cruise. It seemed like a nice way to relax and see the sites from a different angle.

"You look stunning," I said.

Even in the candlelight, I saw her blush.

"This old thing?" she said with a chuckle.

Suggested dress for the dinner cruise was more formal than anything either of us had, so we went shopping. I purchased a suit within a half hour, but Elsie dragged London from boutique to boutique until they found the perfect dress. And I have to say, the end result was worth the extra effort.

"I didn't say anything about the dress. *You're* stunning."

The corner of her mouth curled up.

"Thank you."

She took a sip of wine, obviously uncomfortable. I'll have to make sure to compliment her more often so she gets used to it.

"So, what was your favorite thing in London?" I asked.

"Oh gosh, I don't know." She looked at the city beyond the panoramic windows. "If I had to pick just one, I'd have to say the Tower of London. It gives a lot of bang for the buck. There's a lot to see there, so much history. But honestly, I loved it all. Thank you for bringing me."

"Trust me when I say, it has absolutely been my pleasure." I looked toward the window and back at her. "Would you prefer to stay here and enjoy the view or head upstairs to the deck?"

"Why don't we check out the deck? We can always come back here."

We walked hand in hand up the stairs and found an empty spot at the railing. I stood behind London and rested my hands on her waist.

"Are you chilly?"

"A little bit." I removed my suit coat and placed it on her shoulders. "Thank you."

She leaned back against me and I wrapped my hands around her waist.

"It's a nice view from here."

She nodded.

"When you're out there, it's so full of energy and life, and the kaleidoscope of sights and sounds could be distracting. From this vantage point, you see everything without all that noise."

She's always so easy-going, sometimes I forget all she's been through in her young life. I can't imagine losing either one of my parents. And here she is, two years younger than me, and she's lost both. Perhaps that's the reason she has a maturity to her I haven't seen in other women her age.

There's so much I'd like to say, but I don't want to ruin this moment. It's too peaceful. So instead, I enjoyed the sound of the water below, the stars twinkling in the inky night sky above, and the feel of London in my arms.

I don't know how long we stood like that, before I felt her take in a deep breath and let it out.

"I love it here," she said. "Not just London. This country. I feel so at home."

A warm sensation spread through my chest at her words. I took a minute to collect my thoughts then kissed the top of her head and turned her to face me.

"I love you here," I said. "I love *you*."

It took her a second to process my shift in meaning. When she did, her eyes widened then filled with tears. I held my breath, awaiting her response. It seemed like we stood there, looking at each other forever. Finally she smiled.

"I love you, too."

She blinked and a tear escaped. I wiped it away and cupped her cheek.

"Then why are you crying?"

"Because I'll be leaving." She sniffed. "And I know how much living without someone you love hurts."

I felt sucker punched by those words. Obviously I know our time together has an expiration date. Namely the one listed on her plane ticket home, but it's not something I want to think about. I may be in denial, but I believe that somehow this will all work out.

Cupping her jaw, I used my thumbs to dry her tears and did the only thing I could think of that would comfort us both. I placed my mouth over hers and kissed her.

Chapter Nine

"THAT CASTLE IS AMAZING." I said.

Today, we took the four-hour journey to Cornwall to tour St. Michael's Mount. It's a tidal island, connected to the mainland by a cobbled causeway that's only accessible at low tide. We were able to walk over on the way here, but may end up taking the ferry back.

"You do love castles."

"Probably because we don't have many of them back home."

"As you've seen, we've an abundance of them here."

"And they're so cool. Can you imagine living in one?" He flashed an I-know-something-you-don't smile. "What?"

"Nothing." He shook his head. "And no, I can't imagine living in one. It seems drafty."

"Bundling up would be worth it."

We toured the castle, chapel, and gardens and decided to take a well-deserved break and have a snack at The Island Cafe. It's a little breezy outside, so we opted to sit inside. I like to sample local delicacies and couldn't decide between the Cornish cream tea and Cornish pasty. Ever the voice of reason, Bas said to get both.

While we waited for our food, I looked out the window at the spectacular views.

"You said no castle, but could you imagine living here? On the island?"

"It would be different, but not awful," he said. "Why? Are you planning on moving here?"

I know he meant the question as a joke, but it still packed a punch. We've both been falling more in love as the days pass, ignoring the fact that I have to go home. Thankfully our food was ready before I could think about that more, distracting me from that line of thought.

"This is also something you don't see often in the States." I pointed to the teapot. "Some restaurants have personal-sized pots, but obviously the aesthetic isn't the same."

I filled my cup and set the pot down.

Bas cut his pasty in half while I prepared my scone with clotted cream and strawberry jam. Lifting my master-piece, I took a bite and moaned.

"So yummy." I held it up. "Want a bite?"

"No thank you," he said. "I'm not a fan of clotted cream."

"Seriously?" I pointed toward his Coke. "You don't drink tea or eat clotted cream. They're going to revoke your citizenship."

"I'm eating pasty and I drink ale, so that's got to count for something."

On that note, we finished our meals and prepared to head to the hotel we're staying in tonight. While we'd been exploring, the tide had come in so we walked to the landing to grab the ferry off the island.

Once we crossed the causeway, we made our way back to the car and headed to the hotel. He hasn't been very forthcoming with facts about where we're staying and as we approached, I understood why.

"Is that a *castle*?"

"You've got a keen eye."

I dragged my gaze from the impressive sight in front of me and looked over at him.

"Seriously? We're staying in an actual castle?"

"We are."

A valet greeted us as we pulled under the portico. He opened my door and I stepped out, then retrieved the key from Bas, who was taking the bags out of the trunk.

"Ready?" Bas asked.

I nodded, still taking in the castle and its surrounding scenery.

"This place is a destination in itself," I said as we made our way inside, which was as magnificent as the outside.

The staff greeted us with smiling faces and as they checked us in, I looked around at the stunning furnishings, which were somehow grand and inviting at the same time. As we made our way to our room, I took in the decor. Each detail in the common areas was more refined than the next.

Bas opened the door with an actual key instead of a plastic card and stepped aside for me to enter.

"This is beautiful."

He set the bags down and sat on the edge of the large four-poster bed. I peeked into the bathroom and was happy to find it equipped with both a large steam shower and a claw-foot tub that's easily big enough for two.

"You like it?" he asked when I returned.

I stepped between his thighs and placed my hands on his shoulders.

"I love it."

"I'm glad."

"And I love you."

He wrapped his arms around my waist and pulled me in for a kiss.

"I thought we could eat dinner at the restaurant downstairs and explore the grounds, then maybe get to bed early."

"I have a better idea."

"What's that?"

"Order room service, eat at that table right over there in front of the window, then enjoy a soak in the gigantic tub."

"That sounds like a brilliant plan."

―――――

BAS

PER LONDON'S PLAN, we ordered room service and settled at the small table to eat. Normally she gets a local special, but the sharable surf and turf caught her eye. I'm always game for a bit of steak and lobster, so that's what we ordered.

We're eating a little later than planned. After settling into the room, we decided to shower after our long day touring the island and got a bit distracted. But we also worked up a rather large appetite. The lobster didn't stand a chance, and we managed to tackle a good three-quarters of the gigantic ribeye.

"I hope you saved room for the make-your-own sundae bar you were eyeing on the menu."

"There's always room for ice cream."

I stood and tightened the sash of my robe. After showering, we both donned robes provided by the hotel instead of getting dressed. Mine refuses to stay closed. As I placed the order, I thought about what a pity it is that London's not having the same issue.

"The ice cream will be here in twenty minutes," I said.

She'd already started stacking dishes and I helped her finish. We piled everything on the tray and I set it on the floor outside the door. When I came back inside, London was standing in front of the window, looking at the view.

"Thank you for bringing me here," she said when I stepped behind her.

I kissed the back of her neck then rested my hands on her shoulders and gently massaged.

"You're very welcome."

We stayed just like that, in silence, enjoying the view until a soft knock intruded on the

moment. I let go of her shoulders and gave the back of her head a kiss before heading to answer the door. I took the huge tray from the waiter and carried it inside then set it on the table. Together, London and I removed the lids until all the toppings were revealed.

"I hope you don't mind, but I told them we didn't want any fruit," I said as I reached for a bowl and filled it with two scoops of ice cream then handed it to London.

She shook her head and carried on munching the chocolate chips she'd pinched from the

bowl.

"As long as you got rainbow sprinkles, we're good."

I filled a bowl for myself then sat to add toppings.

"Do they actually taste different than just one plain color?"

"Of course they do," she said as she picked up the spoon and poured hot fudge over her ice cream.

I was about to debate that when she did the same thing with the caramel topping. My cock went from zero to hard remembering the sticky toffee pudding night and what happened after I'd helped her clean caramel from her lip.

To take my mind off things, I turned my attention to creating my own sundae. I chucked a bit of everything into my ice cream because, why the hell not? After placing a dollop of whipped cream on top, I tucked in to enjoy my masterpiece.

"Is this on every room service menu?"

"I'm not sure," I said around a mouthful of ice cream.

"If not, it should be."

I'd just gotten myself under control when she licked her spoon. I'm aware she's just savoring the ice cream and not doing it to rile me up, but regardless, that's what's up happening. By the time we both finished eating, I was hanging on by a thread.

London looked at me and raised her brow.

"What's wrong?"

I stood and dipped my index finger in the caramel then reached out and dabbed it just above her lip.

"You have caramel on your lip."

The corner of her mouth curled up into a sexy smile.

"Would you clean it off for me?"

"Indeed."

Resting one hand on the back of her chair and the other on the table, I leaned toward her and licked at her lips. She curled her hands into the lapels of my robe and pulled me close as our mouths pressed together. As the kiss went on, she stood and stepped forward, forcing me to take a step back. When the back of my legs pressed against my chair, she pushed at my shoulders.

My sash had come untied once again so when I sat, my robe opened revealing my hard cock. She nibbled at her bottom lip and stared at him. When she nodded and our eyes met, I wasn't sure what was coming next, but it sure as hell wasn't what she actually did.

She reached over and picked up the bowl of caramel then dropped to her knees. After resting the bowl on my thigh, she picked up the spoon and proceeded to drizzle caramel over my cock until it was completely covered.

I looked on as she meticulously set the bowl back in its place, my heart racing.

Settling back in front of me, London rested her hands on either side of my thighs and leaned forward.

"Oh look, you've got a spot of caramel on you," she said, her hot breath caressing my overly-sensitized skin. "Let me clean that off for you."

Since all rational thinking had shifted south, it took me a moment to process her words. And by the time I caught on, her mouth was already on me.

A ragged moan escaped me as she licked up one side of my cock and down the other. She looked up and met my gaze as she licked her lips, removing the lingering caramel. I held my breath and watched as she lowered her head and wrapped her lips around me again and alternately sucked and rolled her tongue around the head like it was her favorite sucker.

I curled my fingers into her hair, giving her a warning. "London."

She released me with an audible pop and sat back on her heels. Taking in deep breaths, I fought to regain control, but London is obviously trying to make me lose it. Gently loosening the sash of her robe, she unfastened it before letting it fall behind her. My fingers itched to touch the pert breasts and tight nipples she'd exposed, but before I could, she wrapped her hand around the base of my shaft. As she tightened and loosened her hold, I felt the lingering stickiness from the caramel.

"I guess I didn't work hard enough at removing the caramel," she said. "I promise I can do better."

She leaned forward and pulled me into her warm mouth inch by inch.

"Holy shit."

I curled my fingers into her hair and watched her lick, suck, and stroke me until I couldn't take it anymore, then closed my eyes. But that only made the sensation more intense, so I opened them again.

"London." My voice came out as a low croak, so I said her name again. Instead of stopping, she looked up at me with those bright green eyes. "London, if you don't stop, I'm gonna come."

I swear her mouth curled into a satisfied smile and I *know* she reached up, cupped my balls, and lightly tugged. Tightening my fingers in her hair, I braced myself. She seemed to be on a mission and I'd lost the will to stop her.

Her head bobbed up and down, faster and faster. I was barely holding on when she moved her hand from my shaft and, without her fist as a barrier, pulled me to the back of her throat. I finally let myself go.

Chapter Ten

ONE WEEK. That's all I have left. Since our overnight trip to Cornwall a few weeks ago, time has really started to move fast. Which is strange because we've been doing less. While my first weeks here were action-packed with tours and activities, we've spent these last ones just living a normal life.

We've worked on Bas's cottage and hung out with his friends at the pub. I watched some more cricket matches, and even though Sebastian was there to explain what was happening, I still didn't understand. But that didn't stop me from cheering for Bas and his teammates.

It was almost like we're a normal couple, not one with a firm end date.

Shaking away that last thought, I just finished getting dressed when my phone buzzed on the nightstand. I ran across the room to answer it, then flopped on the bed.

My mood lifted when Aunt Maisie's face filled my

screen. I'd called her earlier when I was feeling low, but she'd been in a meeting.

"Sorry about that before," she said.

"No, I'm sorry for calling in the middle of the workday. Sometimes I forget the time difference."

"Are you okay?"

"Yeah, why?"

Her eyes shifted back and forth as she studied me.

"You look sad."

"No, I'm okay. Things are just getting a little emotional, that's all."

"Because you're leaving?" I nodded. "Is staying an option?"

I know what she's asking.

"It is," I said. "But I have to get back home and find a job."

"Do you?"

"As much fun as I'm having, I do miss home. I miss you and Jackie and Ava," I said. "And besides, I'd have to leave eventually. I can only stay here six months without a visa, if I could even get one."

"What does Bas say?"

"He says we'll figure it out."

"At least you know where you stand with him."

"Yeah."

Bas has asked if I'd consider staying. But like I just said to Aunt Maisie, it's not as simple as that.

My single-word answer must have cued her in on the fact that I don't want to talk about this anymore, so she changed the subject.

"So what are you up to tonight?"

"Bas and I are going out to an early dinner with Sebastian and Sharon. Then I'm going to Sharon's book club with her."

"That sounds fun."

"The book they're discussing was good, so it should be," I said. "What about you? What are you doing this weekend?"

I listened as Aunt Maisie filled me in on her plans, which mostly consisted of events for Ava. For a five year old, she has quite the active social life.

"I'm exhausted just listening to that list," I said.

"Tell me about it." She shifted her eyes away from her phone, then back again. "I have a call starting in five minutes, so I have to go."

"Okay, enjoy."

"Oh yeah, it's gonna be a blast," she said with a chuckle, then turned serious. "Enjoy tonight and this last week."

"I will. Have fun this weekend. I'll talk to you Monday unless something comes up."

We disconnected the call and I walked back into the bathroom to put the finishing touches on my hair and makeup.

The book we're discussing at Sharon's book club tonight is a romance novel. There were so many obstacles thrown at the hero and heroine and they overcame them all to end up with each other. I know it's just a book and being a romance, it has to end with a happily ever after, but it still gives me a tiny bit of hope. Even though I have no idea how, I still want to believe that there's a way for Bas and me to be together.

A couple months ago, my Tiktok feed was flooded with people who manifest. They all swore that if you put out what you want into the universe, it will come to you. I don't necessarily believe in that kind of thing, but I don't totally *not* believe in it either.

I closed my eyes, took a deep breath, and wished for a

future with Bas and a chance to see how our story plays out.

———

BAS

Two days left.

In the span of a blink, three months slipped by. Strangely enough, when Mum tasked me with showing London around, it felt like forever. And now, here I am, longing for more time.

Elsie is coming home tomorrow and Mum is planning one last dinner for London. So tonight is our final chance to spend time alone. I've been in the shower now for fifteen minutes, trying to get my emotions sorted. I want to enjoy tonight, not spend it whining about the fact that she's leaving.

I turned off the water and wrapped a towel around my waist as I stepped out of the shower. A billow of steam followed me as I left the bathroom.

"I was worried you fell asleep in there," London said.

"My shoulders are sore after doing all that yardwork yesterday. The spray felt good."

It's not a total lie. It did feel good, it's just not the main reason I stayed in so long.

London picked her dress off the bed and inspected it.

"I'm going to steam this," she said.

There's no need to ask if she knows where the steamer is, she's used it a few times while staying here. It still surprises me how seamlessly she's fit into my life. We only knew each other a week when she basically moved into the carriage house with me. As if that weren't enough, we spent most of our days together as well.

I walked over to the closet and rummaged inside for

my black trousers and button-down shirt. When I turned around, London was standing behind me, fully dressed. I tossed my clothes on the bed and placed my hands on her waist.

"You look beautiful," I said, pressing a kiss against her forehead.

I'd love to kiss her lips, but she'd meticulously applied her lipstick and I don't want to mess it up.

"Thank you." She looked down at her black dress. "Elsie was right about that other dress, so when she told me to buy this, I listened."

"I'll be ready in two minutes," I said.

After taking one last look in the mirror, she walked out to the living room. I found her transferring money and credit cards into a small clutch purse. She better not think she's paying tonight.

I'll cross that bridge when and if we come to it. Instead of saying something, I grabbed my keys.

"Ready?"

She nodded and we walked out the door. It's a beautiful night, but I'm keeping the top up so her hair doesn't get messed. Maybe it'll still be nice on the way back and we'll be able to drop it. London loves riding with the top down as much as I do.

The restaurant is only a fifteen-minute drive, and before long, we pulled into the parking lot. She looked at the fifteenth-century Tudor cottage.

"This place is so romantic," she said as we entered the building.

The dim lighting, candlelight, and intimate seating give the space the perfect ambiance for a special date. Daniel proposed to Sarah here. That's the kind of place it is.

The hostess seated us at a table for two, tucked into the corner by the fireplace. It's too warm for a fire, but there are lit votive candles scattered along the hearth, offering a cozy glow.

"Word from Daniel is that the scallops served here are beyond amazing." I looked up at her. "That is, if you like scallops."

"I do," she said. "And that's actually something I usually order out because they never turn out as good when I cook them at home."

"Would you like to get a bottle of wine?"

"I'm not feeling much like drinking alcohol tonight," she said. "I had a lingering headache most of the day and I'm just not in the mood."

When the waitress returned for our orders, she asked for ginger ale. I followed her lead and ordered a Coke. We decided to share the spicy crab appetizers with toast points and each asked for the scallop entree.

Once we were alone again, I held up my glass to toast.

"To an amazing night with a lovely lady."

I tapped my glass against hers then took a drink and watched her do the same.

Throughout the appetizer and entree, we discussed a myriad of topics ranging from how silly she thinks the rules of cricket are to the new project I'll be starting next week. One thing we avoided was talking about the fact that she's flying home in two days and I have no idea when or if I'll see her again. We promised each other we'd enjoy our time together without dwelling on the future. I've managed to do it so far, but it hasn't been easy, especially this past week.

We left the restaurant and got back into the car. When I turned in the opposite direction of my parents' house, she didn't even question it. A few minutes later, I pulled into the driveway of the cottage and we walked inside. I followed her up the stairs to the bedroom and bumped into her when she stopped in the doorway.

"Oh Bas, they're beautiful."

I'd set vases filled with English wildflowers throughout the room. While she admired those, I walked around and lit the votives I'd laid out earlier. I turned off the overhead light and the candles cast a soft glow on the golden walls.

I walked over to London and skimmed my fingers along her jaw before tucking a stray hair behind her ear. There's so much I want to say, but I'm going to let my actions speak for me tonight.

Pulling her against me, I lowered my head and opened my mouth over hers. There was no

slow build up, it was just a frantic, desperate kiss between two people who wanted more than anything to turn back time. And as our tongues tangled, and we feasted on each other, in the back of my mind I wondered how someone I'd just met three months ago could taste so familiar.

Reaching down, I cupped her ass and lifted her. She wrapped her legs around my waist and held onto my neck.

My erection brushed against her as I walked across the room. I set her down next to the bed and didn't waste any time removing her dress. Within seconds, she stood in front of me wearing a black lace bra and panty set. I traced my finger along the edge of the underwear.

"This is different."

She shrugged.

"I thought I'd add a little spice."

"These are nice." I reached around and unhooked her bra. "But rest assured, you're the sole spice I crave."

I gestured for her to sit on the edge of the bed and knelt between her thighs. Pulling her forward, I draped her legs over my shoulders then placed my open mouth right at the juncture of her thighs. She curled her fingers into my hair and held on as I alternately licked and sucked her through the lace.

I pulled her underwear off, allowing my tongue to slip between her slick folds and taste her without any barrier. Slipping my middle finger inside her, I pulsed it in and out while circling her clit with my tongue. She arched toward me then fell back onto the mattress, opening herself to me even more, which I took full advantage of.

Her breathing turned into shallow pants as I added my index finger and thrust into her faster and faster and sucked to the same rhythm.

"Bas—I'm gonna—"

Whatever else she said came out as more of a garbled noise than a word.

I curled my fingers and stroked her inside and sucked on her clit at the same time.

"Oh my God!" she screamed as her inner walls clamped down on my fingers over and over again.

I removed my clothes and stepped between her wide-spread thighs. She looked up at me and smiled. I thrust into her and froze, then groaned when she wrapped her legs around my waist.

"Fair warning, this is going to be fast."

I'M nothing if not a man of my word, and four pumps later, I let out a low growl and collapsed on top of her.

Chapter Eleven

LONDON

I SAT in Aunt Maisie's living room coloring with Ava. Of all the activities available, she

chose this one. As I colored a turtle, I thought of Bas's artwork. Yes it's a stretch, but it doesn't take much to bring him to mind.

"Why do you look sad, London?"

I looked at Ava who studied with worried blue eyes. Reaching out, I pulled her into a hug and kissed the top of her head before releasing her.

"How could I be sad when I'm hanging out with you?'

She's a pretty smart kid and didn't buy my non-answer.

"I don't know," she said. "But you look like you're gonna cry."

"Sorry." I blinked away my tears. "Better?"

"No."

One thing you can always count on with kids is an

honest answer. Maybe not about who ate the last cookie, but definitely about how bad you look.

"Why don't you give London a break?" Jackie asked.

"A break from what?"

"From all your questions," Jackie said in a silly voice as she tickled Ava's belly.

When Aunt Maisie announced she was dating a woman four years ago, I'll admit Mom and I were shocked. Not because we think there's something wrong with it, but because up until she met Jackie, she'd only dated men. And she'd had a pretty robust dating life. Some men even graduated from casual date to relationship status. But I suppose there's a reason why none of those lasted.

From what Aunt Maisie says, it was love at first sight for her, but less so for Jackie. But it didn't take long until they were both head over heels. I'm sure Aunt Maisie's love for Ava helped with that.

"I'm so happy you and Aunt Maisie found each other," I said with a sniffle.

"Oh God," Jackie said. "Please don't cry."

"I'm not. I'm just…" I trailed off and shrugged as a tear rolled down my cheek.

"Hold on."

I watched Jackie leave the room with Ava in tow.

"What's wrong?" Aunt Maisie said, a few minutes later. "And if you say nothing, I'm going to tickle you until you spill."

"I had a dream last night that has me all discombobulated."

"About Bas?"

I nodded.

"Ever since returning, I've had the same dream about Bas," I said. "Not a dream really, more like an altered memory of our last night together. He asks me to stay and instead of saying no like I did, I say yes. But this dream was different. Mom was in it."

"What was she doing?"

"Bas and I were at his cottage, which was fully renovated. The doorbell rang and when I opened the door, mom was standing there, wearing that blue dress she always loved." Tears filled my eyes and I blinked them away. "She stepped into the house and pulled me into a hug and said, 'I'm so glad you're here.' And that was it. I woke up." I wiped at my cheeks and looked her in the eyes. "It was so real. I can still feel her hug, smell her perfume."

My tears changed into all-out sobs. Aunt Maisie pulled me against her chest and held me. Once I calmed down, I pulled back.

"I know you probably think I'm overreacting, because it was just a dream."

"I don't think you're overreacting," she said, then after a few seconds of silence added, "Are you going to ask me what I do think?"

I reached for a tissue and blew my nose, then nodded.

"What do you think?"

"I *think* you should go back to England."

Every reason I've already offered for not staying there was on the tip of my tongue, but she anticipated each and every one. Well, all but the last one.

"I'll miss you. You're my family."

I saw tears fill her eyes before she pulled me into another hug.

"Oh honey, you'll always have me." Shifting back, she looked me in the eye. "You owe it to yourself to give this thing between you and Bas a chance."

- "Will you come visit?"

- "Between us visiting you, you visiting us, and
  FaceTime, you'll be sick of looking at

me."

———

BAS

I PUT the moulding into place and cursed. Now it's too short.

"Shit!"

I threw it across the room and walked outside.

The rule is to measure twice and cut once. I've been measuring at least three times and still getting it wrong. That's the third moulding I've wasted. Before that, I messed up a piece of plywood.

- After London left, I worked like a madman,
  tearing this place apart. Putting it back

together is proving more difficult. I suppose the headspace I'm in isn't conducive to precise work, but there's no more demo to do.

I dragged my fingers through my hair and willed myself to calm down. Mum is stopping by in a bit and if she sees me in this state, she'll tell me about myself…again.

She thinks I should go after London. Hell, she thinks I shouldn't have let her leave in the first place. But what was I to do? I asked her to stay. She said no. I couldn't very well tie her to a chair.

That line of thinking isn't doing anything to calm me down. I shook my head to clear it and went inside to get a beer, then went back out and sat on the step. Instead of focusing on this house or London, I thought about the project I'm working on. It's a new video game by a small startup. They have good backing and a solid plan. It's just been a slow-go because they're being super cautious since they're working with other people's money. We've had a shit-ton of in-person meetings and right now, I have to get every single line I draw approved.

I took a drink and chuckled.

Well, that last one might be a bit of an exaggeration, but not much of one.

"You know, this house will never get done if all you do is sit out here talking to yourself."

I froze at her voice, afraid to turn around in case I'm imagining it.

"You're not imagining it. I'm here."

I turned and met her uncertain gaze.

"For how long?"

"Hopefully as long as you want me," she said.

She barely finished her sentence and I was up, standing in front of her.

Placing my hands on either side of her face, I said, "I'll want you forever."

"There's some paperwork to fill out, but I'm committed to being here long-term."

I kissed her smiling mouth then pulled back to look at her before pressing my mouth

against hers again. This second kiss was a little less restrained, a lot hotter, and with way more tongue.

When we pulled back again, London and I were both breathless.

"I love you so much, I felt like I was dying without you," I said.

"I love you too, and it was the same for me," she said. "I'm so sorry."

"What for?"

"For leaving."

"No need to apologize for that," I said. "You're here now."

"Hopefully for good," she added with a smile.

"Welcome home."

Epilogue

FOUR MONTHS LATER...

"LONDON, ARE YOU NEARLY READY?" Bas asked from downstairs. "I need help with something."

"I'll be right down," I said.

Hopefully it's nothing messy since I'm already dressed. I finished applying mascara then brushed and sprayed my hair. After making sure there was no paint lingering on my face or anywhere else, I turned off the light and left the bathroom. I slipped into my shoes and headed downstairs.

I couldn't stop a smile from forming as I descended the stairs. Over the past months, Bas and I have worked nonstop to finish renovations on the cottage. We finished our last task today, which was putting a final coat of paint on the downstairs rooms.

The space looked just like it had in my dream and I'm absolutely in love with it. Almost as much as I'm in love with the man staring out of the window in the living room.

"I'm ready to go."

"You look lovely," he said.

"So do you." I looked at my dress. "Are you sure what I'm wearing is okay?"

He'd gotten dressed and left the bedroom while I was in the shower, so I hadn't seen what he'd put on. I'm a little surprised to see him in a suit and tie. Sunday dinner at his parents' house isn't usually a super formal occasion.

"You're fine." He stepped forward and took my hands in his. "I want to talk to you about something."

My stomach twisted at his serious tone.

"Is something wrong?"

"No. Everything is perfect." He leaned down and placed a soft kiss on my lips then pulled back. "You're perfect."

I looked around the room, trying to figure out what's going on. He said he needed help with something, but I can't see what.

"What did you need help with?"

"I have a question that only you can answer." He took in a deep breath and let it out. "London Spencer, when my mother suggested that I take on the role of your tour guide, I was a bit unsure about what I was getting into. However, the instant I set eyes on you, there was a connection, and it's blossomed into something truly wonderful. When you left, I felt adrift, uncertain of how to carry on. Then, when you returned, I made a vow to do everything in my means to bring you joy...and to make sure you never leave again," he added with a smile.

My heart pounded as he dropped down to one knee and I realized what was happening.

"So I'm asking you to make me the happiest man in the world." He pulled a box out of his pocket and opened it then held it up. "Will you marry me?"

"Yes." I dropped to my knees and wrapped my arms around his neck. "Yes, I'll marry you."

He pulled back slightly and removed the ring from the box. My hand shook and he steadied it as he slipped the ring onto my finger.

"Perfect fit."

He kissed the back of my hand, then pulled me up to stand.

"Bas, this ring is gorgeous."

I moved my hand back and forth, watching the light from the window play against the diamond. The engraved details on the side of the white gold band give it an old-fashioned look that I love.

"I'm glad you like it," he said. "I researched vintage rings and sketched out this design by combining elements from a handful that stood out. The local jeweler brought it to life."

"You designed this?" He nodded. "Now I love it even more."

I pulled him down for a kiss, but Bas ended it before things got too heated.

"Hold that thought until later," he said. "We need to leave for my parents'. Mum will be in party mode and drive everyone crazy if we're late for dinner."

As we drove the short distance to his parents' house, I stared at my ring, trying to convince myself that this is real. It feels like a dream.

Bas pulled into his parents' driveway and we got out of the car. I felt like I was floating as I walked next to him. He opened the door and stepped aside for me to enter. I'd expected Sharon to be in the kitchen in full party mode, but the room was empty and the house was eerily quiet.

I looked over my shoulder at Bas.

"Where is everyone?"

"They must be in the dining room."

We walked in there, but while the table was set, the room was empty. I followed him into the living room and jumped back as I heard a chorus of "Congratulations!"

My heart pounded and I blinked.

"Am I hallucinating?'

Along with Sharon, Sebastian, and Elsie, Aunt Maisie, Jackie, and Ava stood in the middle of the room holding champagne flutes.

"Surprise!" Bas said from behind me.

"They all knew about this?" I asked him. He nodded. "You all knew?"

Sharon stepped forward and pulled me into a hug.

"We did and we're thrilled."

Sebastian and Elsie followed suit and then Jackie and Ava did the same. The last one to approach was Aunt Maisie. Her image blurred and I blinked her into focus.

"So when I was talking to you last night and you said you couldn't FaceTime…"

"I was already here." She wrapped her arms around me and squeezed me tight. "I'm so happy for you."

I sniffed and nodded, unable to speak. Pulling back slightly, she wiped the tears from my cheeks. Finally I found my voice.

"I have you to thank for this. You convinced me to come on the trip in the first place, then persuaded me to come back."

"This was all your mom." She looked over at Bas. "Although even she couldn't predict how much coming here would change your life." She stepped back. "But enough crying. We have an engagement to celebrate."

Before dinner, I showed everyone my ring. They've seen pictures of it, but I imagine it's more impressive in person. And once we gathered around the dining room table, a lump formed in my throat as I looked around.

Last year, I couldn't imagine ever being this happy. When I got on that plane all those months ago, I had no idea how much the trip would change my life. But here I am, surrounded by family, both old and new.

I looked up at Bas and smiled.

"I love you."

"I love you too, London." He kissed me then smiled back, that dimple popping in his right cheek. "And I can't wait to spend the rest of my life with you."

And for the first time in a long time, I didn't fear the future.

The End

Join Tina's newsletter and receive a free book!

https://dl.bookfunnel.com/gk3tnp52pu

9 781961 539082